FOOTPRINTS
ON MY
Mirror

FOOTPRINTS ON MY *Mirror*

J. GRACE WARREN

To order additional copies of this book, contact:
Bookwhip
1-855-339-3589
https://www.bookwhip.com

FOOT PRINTS ON MY MIRROR

Do you believe in dreams, angels, omens, old wives' tales, or superstitions? Jolene and her son Marlon did not until they both experienced some strange happenings that made them doubt their sanity at times.

Experiencing any of those can be a frightening ordeal but imagine having a sick child being treated in a medical institution for an unfamiliar illness and having no knowledge whatsoever of the end result of the treatment, whether it be recovery or death.

CHAPTER

1

The month of May heralds the coming of the long awaited summer on Bluehole Cove, a tiny island tucked deep somewhere among the islands of Northern and Southern Pacific Ocean, where the skies lend their hue of aqua blue, and sea breezes sing a lullaby swaying the majestic coconut palm trees to and fro. Only a few people in the rest of the world enjoyed relaxing in the peace and quiet of that cove.

The TWENTY-EIGHTH day of MAY is the National Holiday on the island, celebrated every year with a parade, parties and a free-for-all dance in the night to end the day's activities.

The celebrations commence with a ceremony in the morning at which the Governor arrives escorted by police officers amidst cheering crowds, followed by many dignitaries. He inspects the military troops, fire fighters and police officers. Other organizations present are not inspected. Blessing of the land and its inhabitants is said by a clergyman; local songs and musical items are rendered and the State of Affairs address is given by the Principal Secretary to the Governor. At the conclusion of the ceremony the Governor exits the scene accompanied by police escorts, followed by a motorcade of dignitaries. Every year a theme is selected for the celebration like: "KEEP BLUEHOLE COVE CLEAN," or "SAVE SEA CREATURES" like Walloby the humpback whale. The celebration continues with the national parade, beach parties and church bazaar to fill the agenda for the rest of the day. The uniformed organizations led by a moderate military marching band, parade proudly through the narrow streets of Bluehole Cove, dispersing at separate headquarters; the citizens following behind marching to the beat of other bands.

A generous assortment of ingenious sea creature floats graced the occasion: beautiful red snapper, a float with a variety of little gold and other kinds of fish. A turtle, a sea star, dolphin, shark, a whale, and many mollusks: lobster, conch, crawfish, shrimp, oyster. Those were followed by a group of sea horse, jelly fish, sea serpents, and the beautiful blue and purple man-o-war. A 'wish willy' or lizard float. Little thatched houses like the ones on the beach mounted on a wooden slab, all transported by different means; beautifully and meticulously made.

The streets are lined with "papta" or palm trees, and decorated with red, white, and blue streamers and little union jack flags. The uniformed organizations disperse and the parade transforms into dancing in the streets island style, with island music blaring, and every able body dancing, some dressed in sea creatures costume, while some in what Mrs. Tradis, a senior citizen well known for her outspokenness would say "somebody call the police, they should be arrested", and making moves that was never seen before on that island, expressing themselves they called it, 'making rather merry,' as Bob Crotchet told Mr. Scrooge. May month is generally hot but bearable, ninety and above degrees, with light sea breezes blowing. Parading in sweltering heat is not comfortable but citizens would not be deterred. Along the parade route vendors save the day, selling cold water and cold refreshing fruit drinks. Some in the parade and spectators would carry a bottle of ice water. It would not last very long in temperature like this (needless to say).

On that day beach lovers crowd the beaches picnicking, swimming, playing games, or just sun-bathing on the soft white sands. Some goes fishing and serve up a wonderful fish-fry and Johnny cake dinner. Giant lobsters and beautiful blue crabs running from ship to shore, frolicking on the white sandy beach before their demise, in a whale of a pot of boiling water. Drinks of all sorts to include 'Rum Bumper', a blend of locally brewed, fresh seaweed extract, coconut extract with coconut water and rum cocktail, which according to old wife's tales, was first concocted by early settlers to the island, for healing certain illnesses, and enhance the effectiveness of the drink for sterility in the male population.

Girls in beholding swimsuits that Mrs. Tradis, regarding herself to be Mrs. Prim and Proper, would say for them too, "somebody call the police, they ought to be arrested", parading the length of the island, drawing attention to themselves, and to every eye on the beach; the men drooling with desire.

Sailing sloops cruise lazily along miles of roaring barrier reef, in a betting race to win a gallon of what became the National drink, 'Rum Bumper'.

The more athletic men displayed their muscular physique, capering to keep their ski on top of the waves. To end the day's celebration, a free-for-all dance is held in the night, under in the light of the full moon shining radiantly on the waters. Sometimes before the moon rises high in the sky that night, a shower of refreshing rain falls making the temperature more comfortable. The people would say the moon is washing its face.

People came from all the neighboring islands to celebrate with them. They attend the ceremonies, march in the parades, some in costumes, others just enough clothes to beat the heat. Dancing on the island was always a big event, especially when it was a formal occasion attended by dignitaries. The free-for-all dance was just what it said, free: every able body old and young was there kicking up their heels, having a wonderful time, but it wouldn't go without someone having too much Rum Bumper and creates a brawl.

CHAPTER

2

The people of Bluehole Cove island believed strongly in dreams and all the ancient taboos and Jolene a highly intelligent citizen was no different. She entertained a dream of Bluehole Cove being transformed into a viable productive island, economically independent, and become a beacon of hope to the surrounding islands with less developmental opportunities. How and when that could be, she had no idea. She didn't have even an inkling of promoting such a venture but her dream was about to materialize.

Jolene in her mid-twenties expecting her first baby, was elated at the idea of being a mother. Being an industrious and creative woman, she enjoyed cranking up the handle of her mother's old Singer sewing machine, making her baby's layette and other items for herself. Strangely she was a staunch believer of the superstition that; if two friends are pregnant at the same time, when one delivers, the other waiting to deliver, should not see her friend's baby or one would die. That was enough to scare her, knowing Maggie her friend for 17 years, was expecting her first baby too, and had delivered a girl. Curious to see Maggie's baby Jolene forgot all about the saying and did not heed the superstition; she saw the baby. Superstitious as it was, unfortunately Jolene's baby was born with a very debilitating incurable condition.

The day after the celebrations, preparations for the Church fair organized by Jolene's mother Mrs. Armenia Tradis, dubbed 'Head Cook and Bottle Washer', and the 'busy beavers': Mrs. Frances Shavalria, Miss Babsey Bangles, Miss Lucinda Wilkins a spinster, next door neighbor, alias "The Old Bat", all from the Women's League, and Jolene's aunt Agata Grayday, her mother's sister and Jolene, all clustered in Mrs. Tradis' what was not considered a gourmet kitchen but well organized; 'cooking up a storm' as the saying goes, and decorating the party halls and yard.

After a long and tedious day helping the women's league prepare for the church fair, Jolene in her state of motherhood, waiting to deliver, laid her exhausted body across her rather modest but comfortable bed, with the intension to nap just a few minutes, but fell into third dimension sleep.

With the sound of the roaring reef embedded in her mind, vision of a great big dinosaur having four heads with white human faces, two males and two females of unknown origin, rose up out of the sea, walked to the shore and stood in the center of the soft sand street; she was not afraid. How strange she thought when she awoke.

She mentioned her dream to her grandmother Emisha McFarlyn, who instantly interpreted it to mean that Bluehole Cove would be inhabited by foreigners but didn't know what their mission would be. Jolene wondered if it could be remotely possible that their mission would be to bring progress to the island. She jumped for joy at the thought, visualizing her dream come through.

It wasn't very long before wealthy foreigners settled on the island indeed, and gradually recreated it. Large industrial companies made extensive investments, changed, and modernized the entire island. Bluehole Cove was no longer just a place for rest and relaxation.

Six o'clock in the evening Bluehole Cove lights up all over the island with lights so dim, they looked like fireflies. They were replaced with bright lights that seemed to the inhabitants like glaring light, although they were just the most commonly used, high pressure sodium lamps, which strewed the streets, and lighted homes, sprinkled here and there on the highways.

New homes were built in the latest designs, equipped with the most modern appliances, new gadgets, and indoor plumbing. However, the idea of having the outhouse inhouse did not sit well with them but considering the benefits and conveniences to derive from it, they readily vowed to put it to good use.

Communicating by a new telephone system they can see and talk to each other, and they can see the world through the eyes of television, were all so very amazing.

A modern hospital well equipped with all the necessary provisions, including elevators and modern ambulances, most needed pharmacy replaced the outdated General Hospital pharmacy. Small clinics with pharmacy were made accessible around the town and rural areas.

Tall commercial buildings strewn the main streets and modern electronic machines of every kind was installed. New school buildings and colleges were established around the island. Trading with the outside world showed much progress.

The most modern model cars, and street cars with bellowing horns to alert pedestrians of oncoming traffic were introduced to the inhabitants. Crafted designed bicycles with bells, were the convenient and affordable means of transportation to those who were not ready for the adventure of buying or operating a car. It was the means of transportation for the children also. They operated them with style, showing off their fancy moves and racing. They felt clever riding in and out of traffic, ringing their way through jaywalking pedestrians going every which way.

A small commercial and cargo service, single engine Cessna aircraft they named Cove Wings 1 and 2, was installed with all modern equipment in a Non-towered airport, to service them from Caye to Caye. Palm trees and Blue glow-in-the-dark stones decorated the walkway to the door. Life had really come to Bluehole Cove.

CHAPTER

3

With the celebrations behind them, still working intensely to complete the preparation for the church fair the following day, and chattering like a bunch of cackling hens, none of the ladies noticed Jolene slumped over, experiencing some abdominal discomfort. She did not want to create a scene, so she disappeared quietly to her room to prepare the layette she had made for her baby and trying to decide whether she should pay a visit to the midwife. Unknown to her, Lindsy her baby's father, was having some abdominal discomfort also with unknown cause.

It seemed like that was the only consideration for the night when: "Ouch!" Jolene shouted.

"What was that?!" Mrs. Wilkins "The Old Bat" asked. She hears everything.

"Oooo! Whooo! Jolene moaned again holding the bottom of her belly. "It feels like somebody is performing surgery on me without anesthetic. I think it's time." Those sounds got the attention of the busy group, and almost everyone was running around to ensure that Jolene was well prepared. However, Jolene's mother Armenia Tradis continued the food preparation and did not participate in the excitement. She did not condone Jolene's pregnancy without the sanctity of marriage, and she therefore would not engage herself in her affairs.

Nine months had passed and the long awaiting the birth of her baby had come to an end. Being her first baby, Jolene knew very little about the process of birthing, and that the 'Oooos and Whooos' were only the mere beginning of things to come.

The pain went away, and she was able to make some preparations. Time went by slowly. She thought she had time to finish the preparation and relax until the next pain came, but it wasn't long before she was moaning and groaning again.

The whoooings went on for about three more times before she decided it was time to pack her bag for the journey to Mrs. Robertson the midwife, and so she did.

Lindsy was always attentive and sympathetic to her feelings throughout her pregnancy; making sure she kept in good health; exercised, walking, rest and being comfortable. He was always ready to answer the call.

Attempting to alert him of her readiness to deliver, she scouted every nook and cranny to find him without success. Ironically, he was nowhere to be found at the time of need, therefore she engaged her aunt Agata Grayday to accompany her to the midwife's home. Surprisingly, not too many cars were operating in the dead of night, therefore they were compelled to walk, stopping at intervals with every contraction. It took them approximately half an hour or more to get to Mrs. Robertson's home. It seemed like miles away although they only had to walk two blocks away from her house, cross a bridge, and walk another two short blocks on the other side of the city to Mrs. Robertson's house, a distance she could have walked and be there in twenty minutes, had she not been in that condition.

In the still of the night Jolene could hear herself thinking about the pain as they intensified and came more frequently.

It was late in the night when Jolene and Aunt Agata appeared at Mrs. Robertson's home. She knocked on the door and was greeted by Mrs. Robertson, a tall, fair skin Midwife with long black braids that twisted in the back of her head to form a circle or a 'bun' as ladies called it. She was dressed in her white nurse's uniform, just getting home from visiting one of her patients who had delivered that week.

"Jolene! What are you doing here so late?" Nurse Robertson asked her in a scolding tone of voice, as if she and Aunt Agata committed an unpardonable crime.

"Don't tell me the little one is ready to see the world" she said in a more comforting tone.

"I'm sorry to be here so late, I thought I had more time to think about it, but I see time and tide and baby waits for no man." Jolene answered.

"This is my aunt Agata Grayday, my mom's sister", Jolene said introducing her aunt to Nurse Robertson.

"Good to meet you Mrs. Grayday. Jolene is fortunate to have you accompany her at this time of night.

"Come in, come in" she invited them.

"I think he or she is ready, so I brought my bag to be prepared" Jolene told her.

"These little people coming out these days have a mind of their own" her aunt Agata added.

"Yes! they do!" Nurse Robertson agreed. "Well, come in, come in." She invited them in again.

After her preliminary examination, Nurse Robertson removed her gloves and as she washed her hands over the sink, she turned her head and said, "I don't think he or she will be going anywhere tonight. I say tomorrow at the earliest. You might as well go back home and take a big dose of castor oil and you will be really ready when you come back. Okay? I'll drive you home." she offered.

Now anyone who has taken castor oil will want to know if she took it. Well! Yes! she took it. Believe it or not she took the Midwife's advice, and within a few hours, she was ready for the rest of things to come, still not knowing what to expect.

The evening wore on, and the beavers, still busy in the kitchen, were not aware that it was approaching midnight, and that Jolene having taken the castor oil, was showing signs of being 'really ready' to deliver her baby then.

"Whooo! That was a good one!" Jolene announced, as a strong contraction pain gripped her abdomen. "Castor oil sure works. Think I'd better get back to Nurse Robertson, fast."

The nurse examined Jolene again, and this time she was as ready as she would ever be. Nurse Robertson really knew her business.

The hours dragged on, and so did the pains. Jolene felt like she would spend the rest of her life in birthing pains, each one more intense than the previous one, but she was able to fall asleep for a little while between contractions. It was late in the night, past Aunt Agata's bedtime, so she decided to leave Jolene in Nurse Robertson's care and left the home. Another contraction interrupted that sleep, and unable to be still, she walked round and round in the room. She could have used some encouragement from Lindsy, who was still working at the cabinet shop unknown to her. His career was Mechanical Engineering, but he enjoyed carpentry making hand-crafted wood articles.

Lindsy and his parents Beryl and Rayford Bellfry, lived on the west side of Snodown, a city labeled 'the wrong side of the city', because of its undesirable reputation for crime. His father Rayford worked as a Stevedore, loading and unloading cargo for the ships docking in port, laden with goods. Beryl made a living caring for elderly and disabled citizens.

Lindsy never got around to introducing Jolene to his parents. Like many men, he never got around to doing a lot of things he was supposed to do. He also didn't think it necessary to tell them about the bedroom set he was making for Jolene and the baby, because for a long time he had been promising to make them a set.

Not being from the same side of the tracks as Jolene, Lindsy was hesitant to make their acquaintance with Jolene, knowing Beryl was not easily pleased, and would have made life a bit difficult for everyone. By mere chance she got word of Jolene, who she is, and just as Lindsy predicted, she made a big fuss accusing him of being ashamed of them and vowed to put an end to their relationship one way or another.

CHAPTER

4

The sun rose higher and higher. Suddenly it seemed like ages turned to minutes. Jolene heard of many experiences about the birthing process and had a better idea of what to expect. Signs of actual delivery started to show; a trickle of fluid indicating that her water had broken. Intense pains at shorter intervals got the better of her, and she was now forced to get back to bed in preparation to deliver.

Nurse Robertson prepared all the necessary instruments and examined her again to determine the stage of the delivery. A more intense contraction caused Jolene to squeal like a pig; her face dripping with perspiration in the seventy-five degrees temperature.

"I can't do this Nurse!"

"Please nurse, please take me" she pleaded.

"Take you where child, take you where?"

"Take me anywhere. I don't care, as long as this pain stops."

The pain subsided and she was grateful to be able to take another short nap.

Ten minutes was as long as she would have before a more intense pain woke her up, sending her into the final stage. Approaching the height of the birthing, Nurse Robertson instructed Jolene to start pushing; an instruction that came in time for the pain.

Nurse Robertson was most gentle and sympathetic as she instructed and advised Jolene throughout the delivery.

"Whoooo!" Jolene moaned again, squirming out of position.

"Put your heels down and push yourself back up to the bed head. Now bear down like you are having a bowel movement. Go ahead! Push! Push!" Nurse Robertson urged. Jolene pushed as much as she could.

"I can't do this! I'm not as brave as I thought!" Jolene confessed.

"Yes! You can! You're doing fine! Rest a bit now, you must be ready for the next one," Nurse Robertson told her meaning the next pain. We're almost there, I can feel the head".

Tired, Jolene laid down, but the next pain came, and she had to start pushing again. Her face became flushed and fixed in a grin that made her look like a fierce animal.

"Here it comes! Here's the head!"

"Push again, push!" the nurse kept instructing and lubricating to make the process easier.

Being in labor all those hours exhausted Jolene, and made her slip into a misty world, but she could hear the midwife saying: "Just a little bit longer, and it will be all over."

"With another break and all the strength, she could muster up, Jolene pushed and ended the long birthing journey. She was so right she murmured. Baby came to the world minutes before eight o'clock that morning.

"You have a little girl - a beautiful little girl" Nurse Robertson announced.

"Oh joy! It's over!" Jolene thought. Relief finally came.

Nurse Robertson examined the baby to be sure everything was alright.

"She appears very normal and healthy" she told Jolene. She has ten little fingers; ten little toes; two eyes; two ears; a nose; a mouth; and the biological distinction of gender. All seem in place and intact.

"What was that last one?" Jolene asked curiously.

"The biological distinction of gender, you know, the part that tells that it's a girl" the nurse said jokingly.

"Never heard it put that way before" Jolene said with a little smile. Relief swept through her tired, aching body as she watched the midwife clean and weigh her baby. She weighed five pounds four ounces. Not big, but well worth it she thought. The birth Register book was presented for her to sign and date, which she did without Lindsy the father, present. "The baby's birthday is the same as the date of the National Holiday, the TWENTY-EIGHTH day of May, not easy to forget" she said.

The pain then went away and replaced by the beautiful little being that would change her life forever.

"Have you decided on a name for her?"

"Yes! Her name is Marisa!"

"That is a pretty name. I like it," Nurse Robertson complimented wearily, the result of a long night taking its toll on her too.

Jolene and Marisa were dressed and fed, and Marisa was placed in a tiny crib next to Jolene's bed, so that she could watch over her. They both were so tired they went fast asleep.

Later that day Jolene was awakened by Marisa's cry. Well rested she got up, ready to start her new life as a mother, unaware of an invasion by visitors in the living room, curious about her journey into the wonderful world of motherhood. Aunt Agata had returned bringing with her Jolene's younger sister Ruth, and the misplaced Lindsy she had found leaving the carpenter shop, where he engages in wood crafted articles. He worked diligently through the night on a set of bedroom furniture for Jolene and the baby, not knowing that he was being sought after. He did not know Jolene was at the Midwife's home and had delivered his baby. Marisa's needs attended to, Jolene welcomed the group and introduced Marisa to them. With all the attention she was receiving she got fussy and cried, so Jolene hushed her back to sleep.

Lindsy apologetically tried to explain his where-about of the night before; the reason for him not being present to hold Jolene's hand, to wipe her perspiring brows, and encouraging her on; to be the first to hold his baby, but after all, the custom was that fathers were not allowed in the room to witness the birth, but was expected to be there for support, therefore Lindsy was safe on that point.

Jolene didn't wait to hear from Lindsy what the likely story would be. "You were very attentive through the nine months, taking care of us, making me believe you would be there for the rest of our lives, but failed miserably at the appointed time" she told him in an unpleasant voice.

Jolene's mother Mrs. Armenia Tradis, having a hard time accepting Jolene's decision to become a mother out of wedlock, declined Aunt Agata's invitation to visit Jolene and the baby. Mrs. Wilkins though, 'Old Bat', made her appearance, joining the little gathering to welcome baby Jolene with a neatly wrapped baby wearable blanket or Tote Coat with a matching Tote Bag, both with attached diaper changing pad she had made for Marisa, and a pair of house slippers for Jolene.

Nurse Robertson well rested also, and in a jovial mood, walked into the room and introduced herself. Contributing to the conversation mimicking Jolene, she rehearsed the scene of the night saying:

"Please nurse, please take me!"

"Take you where child, take you where?!"

"Take me anywhere. I don't care, as long as this pain stops."

The visitors were amused. They laughed and laughed all having a comment mocking her.

"Now yo wah noh how baaley grow!' Now you'll know how barley grows" Aunt Agata told her, meaning she will know what it takes to be a mother.

"What it's like to be up all night, nursing a sick child and have to work next day. Mrs. Wilkins told her.

"I'm sure I'll survive until, and after she has grown."

"We thought you were more woman." Ruth told Jolene.

"I did it, anyway, didn't I?"

"You had to. That is one of the things you have to do in life, to bring forth a child, one way or another, as long as it has been conceived."

"No changing your mind on that one my dear." Nurse Robertson told her.

"Think you're more woman brave enough now to do it again?" Lindsy teased. Being the proud and responsible father, he regarded himself to be, even though he was missing in action on this particularly important occasion, was ready to place another order.

"Now that I'm experienced knowing the procedures and expectations, I would do it again depending on where life takes us from here" Jolene told him most assuredly, looking at him with questioning eyes for a reaction, and waiting expectantly for comments from her visitors, but they all refrained from expressing their honest opinion, thinking of Lindsy, not being there for Jolene and his baby.

Fairs, races, parades, picnics all the events of the celebration were discussed. Jolene could only imagine the fun she missed that day but consoled herself saying: "I have a beautiful baby girl, that's better than fairs, picnics or parades, but she was interested to hear about the day anyway.

"How were the celebrations, parade, beach parties, come-one-come-all, free for all dance and so on?" she enquired.

"Just beautiful!" Ruth told her. "It was quite a scene with all the different marching bands and organizations in their prestigious uniforms; crowds following after them with island music blaring and everybody dancing 'making rather merry' like Bob Crotchet told Mr. Scrooge when he returned to work after Christmas" she told Jolene dancing round and round the room.

"We are still at Mrs. Robertson's nursing home you know" Aunt Agata reminded Ruth who gets fired-up just thinking about the music; she so loved to dance, especially to island music.

Taking control of herself she continued to describe the events and the parade.

"The streets were lined with "papta" palms, red, white and blue streamers and little union jack flags."

"I can remember when we used to buy little paper jack flags to pin on our clothes or hats, for two cents" aunt Agata giving them a spec of history.

"The Theme of the parade was "PRESERVE SEA CREATURES". It featured Walloby the humpback whale. An interesting assortment of sea creature floats included: fish - a beautiful red snapper and a variety of little gold and other kinds of fish. Also, a sea star, a turtle, dolphin, shark, a whale, and mollusks: lobster, conch, crawfish, shrimp, oyster. Those were followed by a group of sea horse, jelly fish, sea serpents, and the beautiful blue man-o-war and so on, all beautifully and meticulously done" Ruth said giving Jolene a full and complete description of the parade, then she stopped. Everyone sat silent thinking she was all explained out but she was not.

"Oh!" She just kept going on. "There was also a beach with white sand, coconut trees, sea grapes, cocoplum and even a 'wish willy' a large lizard", not an iguana. Ruth continued then rested long enough to catch a breadth running low on fuel; and of course, there was a mermaid queen perched on a sloop, with a seaweed crown decorated with flowers also; very nice".

"What was the heat like?" Jolene asked.

"Hot! Bearable! Sometimes with a pleasant sea breeze blowing, about 10 miles from the north; she even became the weatherwoman for the day. The regular vendors along the streets with refreshing exotic lemonade, pineapple, and your sea grape drink", cold sky juice – actually rainwater (island talk) saved the day, and the famous intoxicating "Rum Bumper".

"There is nothing like a cold bottle of fermented sugar cane blood builder to beat the heat; my favorite drink" Lindsy interjected.

Knowing what he was referring to, and not being pleased with him without a feasible explanation for neglecting Jolene and the baby, they all just forced a smile without comment. Sensitive as he was, he recognized the cold response to his input and left the room, knowing they were not pleased with him.

All the chattering woke Marisa with a yell that reached clear across the adjoining room. It was time to attend to her needs again, so the visitors were excused, and Marisa was made comfortable, changed and fed.

Lindsy now a first-time father, realizing that he needs to bond with Marisa, and explain his absence to Jolene, thought the time to start was then and there, at that very moment, and returned to the room to be with them.

"Nurse, he addressed Mrs. Robertson, may I hold my daughter for a minute?"

"Most certainly!" she said putting Marisa into his arms.

Receiving the baby Lindsy looked at her for a few minutes, wondering what apologetic words he could say to her, and what explanation he could give to Jolene that would merit forgiveness.

"My precious little angel: Daddy is sorry he wasn't here to see his little angel make her way into this hard but wonderful world, but I promise I'll be close to you always. He kissed her forehead twice then returned her to Nurse Robertson.

Ruth and Aunt Agata left the home but Lindsy stayed on longer, realizing his responsibility of fatherhood is to his 'now family', he would start with his explanation of his absence that he thought could merit forgiveness, and not jeopardize his relationship with them both.

"Jolene, you may not want to believe my explanation for not being here when I should have been" he said, getting straight to the truth, "but I have been working secretly at Buxy's cabinet shop, making a set of bedroom furniture for you and Marisa's room. It was supposed to be in place when you returned home."

Thinking how she had embarrassed him in the presence of company, hang her head in shame for the way she attacked him, without giving him the benefit of an explanation. Feeling foolish she silently started to eat her 'humble pie'. It was her turn to apologize.

"That is a very kind and thoughtful idea. We will always be grateful, I'm sorry for my vicious attack" she said, her head hanging low, not making eye contact.

"We'll make things right and move on" he said accepting her apology. His visiting hour ended he left, allowing mother and baby to settled in for the night.

Not condoning Jolene's pregnancy, and being unable to sleep or contain her guilt not participating in the preparation and excitement of the deliverance of her first grandchild, Mrs. Tradis made her way to Nurse Robertson's home alone, first mission the following morning, with apologies in mind for Jolene, and presents in hand for Marisa, she humbly apologized to them.

Surprised but happy to see her mother, Jolene quickly forgave her and made amends. After putting things right, Mrs. Tradis ended her visit promising to return, and to take her rightful place as a grandmother to Marisa, doing all the things grandmas do with their grandchildren. After all they lived under the same roof, how can they keep avoiding each other? Jolene turned away to attend to her baby.

With the races, picnics, fairs, parties, and parade behind them life reverted to normal.

Three days in Nurse Robertson's nursing home was the given time to make sure everything was all right with mother and baby; to give seasoned mothers time to recuperate, and to get a new mother started, therefore Jolene and Marisa were booted out, and her mothering skills and responsibilities put to the test, with her mother Armenia at her side. Lindsy also made good his promise then, to help and be more attentive to them.

Ruth did her share of caring for Marisa for a while, then carried out her plan to live in the United States.

CHAPTER

5

Mothering seemed easy enough to Jolene for the first month. She did everything she knew how with love to care for her baby. A month old she arranged with the Minister of the neighborhood church for Marisa to be blessed or christening as some would rather say. The custom there was, for a girl baby, two Godmothers and one Godfather were required as witnesses. For a boy, two Godfathers and one Godmother.

Jolene made the arrangements selecting a convenient Sunday, for the two Godmothers and a Godfather; it would be a quiet occasion with light refreshments. Ruth her youngest sister's present to Marisa was an elegant christening dress outfit. Bernie one of the Godmothers made a crib cake with baby in it. Kenton the Godfather, and his wife Zelda, gave a set of baby essentials and a generous amount, of diapers. Jolene provided finger sandwiches, pound cake and aerated water known to them as lemonade. It was to be a simple occasion since it was a Sunday and Mrs. Tradis, Jolene's mother who had to be at work, would not have a brawl at any time let alone Sunday. That day was set aside for church worship services.

However, Lindsy not being one to attend church regularly was missing again from the blessing but thought it fun to invite his friends to celebrate, rather than witnessing the blessing of his precious little baby girl. They brought chairs and tables from the bar they frequented to set up in Jolene's yard to play cards and have a few beers.

"I hope you're not vexed with us," one of the less-known men said. "We only want to celebrate with you and Lindsy."

"I'm irked with the intrusion; moreover, I didn't prepare food," Jolene told him.

"No problem!" I will go to find food. Just let us celebrate with you" he said.

"Please?" said another friend.

So, with their gentle persuasion, she agreed to the celebrating. As a tradition all shops and stores were closed on Sundays, so there was no place to buy food.

The friend was gone for at least half an hour and returned with two bags filled with vegetable soup.

"This is all I could find," he told Jolene. "That's all right because I have no intensions to cook a meal."

Jolene opened the cans and dumped the soup into a saucepan, added a few cups of water and some spices, and in ten minutes the soup was ready and served. A combination of soup and beer must be good together she thought, because all the men appeared to be satisfied.

Bernie one of Marisa's Godmothers' present was a baby chamber pot, and the other Godmother's present was a Steiff bear. Before Jolene got the pot present open Lindsy, having too many beers, and being the clown of the day, took the chamber pot and held it up admiring it.

"This is pretty, thank you Bernie" he said with slurring words, and placed it on his head capering around the yard, missing a step or two.

"Wait! I have a better idea!" he said removing the pot from his head, climbed on a table, still capering he announced:

"Hear Ye! Hear Ye!" he shouted to get the men's attention but capering so much he fell over into a tub of ice and water. He got up drenched, cold, and shivering telling the friends:

"Anybody who did not bring a present must put money into this chamber pot". They all laughed at him.

"You just want to be 'FILTHY RIGH'" one shouted back at him, and good friends that they were, all dug deep into their pockets and produced what money they could afford to make a generous present. The crowd was moderately loud, but the game became more intense, and the volume was turned up. That was unacceptable.

Knowing her mother would be home from work any minute, Jolene urged Lindsy to clean up, take his friends and everything they took to the house and leave, but he and his friends had too many intoxicating drinks and would not cooperate when she told him. Mrs. Tradis nearing home, could hear the commotion from a distance, but couldn't tell where it was coming from.

Lindsy and his company were so intoxicated, they didn't see her walk in the gate and stood motionless in disbelief. Observing the mess thy made, music blaring, and loud conversations, cards playing, all sent her into a rage. She was so indignant her rage induced tightness in her chest and dizziness, causing her to faint. She was escorted immediately by paramedics to the hospital for observation. Dr. Elihue Oakwood conducted the observation and found a small blockage in her arteries, causing a mild heart attack.

That made Jolene uneasy with guilt, thinking it could have taken her mother's life. She thought about the omen that says, when a child is born, in the family someone dies. In the case of a female child born, a female adult die. If a male child is born, an adult male die. Apparently, Mrs. Tradis' time had not come, she was released in two days and lived a good time longer. Lindsy and friends left, and all was quiet again.

At the end of the day Jolene reminisced over the events from dawn to dusk.

"That was so funny, so funny." she thought smiling remembering Lindsy's chamber pot acts, and her disappointment for his absence to the delivery, but her mind quickly reverted to more serious times like the beginning of Marisa's life - her birth. How she Jolene, begged Nurse Robertson the midwife, to take her anywhere to ease the pain of childbirth. "I didn't think it would be so much pain, but I thank God and Nurse Robertson who made it possible for me to endure and come through safely" she thought.

CHAPTER

6

Marisa's little body changed day by day. Her skin shredded like a lizard; her umbilical cord dried and fell off; her cries became stronger; she was holding her head up and eating more like an older baby: she was progressing like she should, and Jolene was contented with her progress. At three months old or thereabout, her stool was expected to change to look like yellow split pea soup, but it didn't. From her limited experience caring for family babies, it was a sign that something was wrong. Fear that there could be a serious problem, Jolene became worried, and together with Lindsy took Marisa back to the midwife and voiced their concern.

"Jolene, you have no reason to be so concerned, she will be fine. Just give her some time," Nurse Robertson advised her, and you too Lindsy, watch and wait.

So! Jolene waited a month for that particular change in her, but it didn't come. She thought maybe she was expecting the change too soon, so she waited another month, but still no change in her stool.

Marisa developed a cold. Jolene took her to the doctor who also assured her that there was nothing to worry about.

"You take it in bad weather?" The distinguished-looking, polish Dr. Bushinsky asked in broken English, with a very pronounced accent.

"Sometimes I take her to her grandmother when I go to work. She takes exceptionally good care of her," Jolene explained, trying to rule out any blame Dr. Brushinsky might have had in mind.

"There! See! just a cold! and soon the stool makes change," he said. That was one-time Nurse Robertson didn't seem to know her business Jolene thought, but after all she is a midwife, not a doctor, and even the doctor was unsure of what was happening.

Marisa's cold got worse, and her stool did change to a darker tar-like substance, and the odor was very offensive. According to the books she read, and the babies she had cared for, or watched grow, Jolene knew it was not an ordinary situation, and had to know what was happening to her baby. She had to find answers, the cause, and solutions. Therefore, the obvious source for an analysis was a Pediatrician, so she went in search of one.

After careful examination and numerous questions, Dr. Clarence Carabahall, one of the most respected Pediatricians on the island, calmly said with a bit of uncertainty: "Considering the symptoms, this seems to be a case of 'Cystic Fibrosis'. He then went on to explain what that was, how it was caused by recessive gene, and there was no known cure at that time, but he would try to make Marisa more comfortable. He admitted her in the Bluehole Cove General Hospital. Jolene's heart sank, but knew she had to be strong for Marisa. It was such a rare disease.

There had been only two such cases a few years before on Bluehole Cove island. The babies were twin girls who were related to Marisa, unknown to Jolene.

Marisa had been hospitalized for two months without any progress. The doctors and nurses believing they could make her better, even cured, challenged themselves to find that magic potion that will make it happen.

A team of doctors and nurses including Dr. Edward Armstrong, a geneticist from the United States, traveling around the world on missions of mercy, happened to be in that region, and were invited to visit Bluehole Cove General Hospital. They met with the local doctors and nurses, and Marisa's case was presented to them.

After a lengthy discussion, Dr. Armstrong gave her a thorough examination, and confirmed the symptoms: Congested lungs, dark tar-like foul-smelling stool, always hungry but no weight gained, big beads of sweat. Yes! it was Cystic Fibrosis. A deadly disease with no cure, caused by recessive gene found mostly in Caucasians. He also explained that for the child to be affected, both parents would have to carry the gene.

Nothing could be done! Marisa would die! but Jolene never gave in to the thought of losing her baby, she stood firm and strong, and nothing or nobody could make her think otherwise.

The nurses at the hospital sympathized with her and tried to cheer her up from time to time, teasing her with the idea of getting started on another baby, but the regimented routine that she followed, left little time for anything else.

Her routine was: getting up early in the morning to do her chores; visit Marisa at the hospital to help with her care; then off to work. Sometimes at midday, dinner time on the island, she would rush back to the hospital to see Marisa. Then back to work to await the end of the day, so that she could get to the hospital again. She would stay with her baby until visiting hours was ended. Somehow, she squeezed in a bite to eat before bedtime.

This routine went on for three months. To watch her baby waste away, apparently always in pain, was a lot to bear, but Jolene endured.

Bluehole Cove was known to have sudden intermittent showers, even in the summer months, and into the stormy season.

One night after her usual visit to the hospital taking care of Marisa, Jolene went home, did her chores, and promising herself a good night's sleep, went to bed to enjoy the soothing sound of an intermittent shower passing over. She didn't get time enough even to get a good snore, when an Orderly arrived at her house with a message from the hospital. At his sight she immediately assumed the worse, and without hesitation

dressed and accompanied the Orderly back to the hospital. Marisa seemed like she was near death but survived that night and more.

There was no cure for cystic fibrosis, and the doctor had told her she would live a few years only. The doctors and nurses tried to keep Marisa alive and comfortable.

On her way to work one morning, Jolene went to see Marisa at the hospital. As she entered the door of the children's ward, Nurse Keeting the head nurse, met her at the door somewhat nervous and very apologetic. Immediately Jolene sense that something was wrong; that her baby's condition had worsened, or maybe she had died.

"Good morning Jolene," Nurse Laura Keeting greeted her. "Enjoying this cool seventy degrees weather?"

"Yes! I much prefer it to the nineties!"

"Have a seat for a moment Nurse Keeting offered, trying hard to keep composed, but was unable to hide her nervousness, arranging and rearranging the chairs around her desk for them to sit. However, she was not one to mince words. Once she was over her nervousness she went straight to the problem; after all she had to be calm to deal with such a delicate matter. Without any more hesitation she told Jolene.

"I have to tell you something that isn't good news, and you would have every right to be upset." She told Jolene trying to explain the situation, still a bit nervous not knowing what Jolene's reaction would be. Jolene could not imagine anything else happening to her baby.

"Come with me!" Nurse Keeting told her. Jolene followed her to the corner of the room where Marisa was lying in her crib, under a steam tent, placed over the crib to help keep her lungs clear.

It was monitored by the head nurse in the day, but at night the younger nurses would get a chance to learn about the steam tent treatment. That was monitored by a Matron who runs the wards at intervals. Nurse Keeting slowly lifted one corner of the tent to show Jolene Marisa's feet. Jolene all but fainted, her stomach sickens by the sight. She tried desperately to keep calm as Nurse Keeting explained that the steamer was put too close to the baby's feet and was not adjusted to the right temperature. I'm terribly sorry" Nurse Keeting apologized.

After seeing what Nurse Keeting was so nervous and apologetic about, Jolene thought it probably would have been better if Marisa had died instead of having to live with the pain and agony that was added to her misery.

Her little feet were scorched, swollen and red. She could only look at her mother with pleading eyes, making crying gestures, because no sound would come from her mouth.

Throughout the apologies and explanations, and despite her efforts to be composed, the blood in Jolene's veins boiled with fury. Such a sight did not call for composure. Jolene therefore exploded.

"Who is the idiot that did this? Who? – what? -- How could anybody be so cruel to an already suffering child, fighting for her life?", Tears flowing as she tried to find an answer for the cause of such cruelty, and wanting to use stronger words, but knew that such words were not in her vocabulary, and for the sake of the children in the ward she controlled her tongue.

"Why did this happen to my baby? Was it because the night staff did not know how to operate the steamer? Or were they sleeping on the job? Or because they just couldn't care less as long as they were maybe having juicy gossips going on. Whatever the reason, somebody should be held responsible," she raged.

Marisa, poor baby, was now in more agony and looked like a progeria patient. Her body was so thin; her face looked so old; her cry was so faint. At times, no sound came out.

"I'm very sorry!" nurse Keeting kept apologizing, but that was no good; the damage was done! 'the arrow flown!' one of the things that come not back. In everything that was happening, Lindsy who promised Jolene and Marisa to be with them always, was once again absent. Jolene was disappointed yet again. It was too much for her to bear alone without him to share the grief, and make decisions, or even suggestions. He had become derelict in his responsibilities to them, therefore, she thought it would be better for her to discontinue the relationship but was still hopeful for a change in him.

CHAPTER

7

One morning at the break of dawn, an Orderly was sent to Jolene from the hospital again, to tell her that Marisa's condition had worsened. Without hesitation she was there by her crib, waiting for the expected, while the nurses tried to make Marisa comfortable, and put her mind at ease.

Jolene, watching and waiting for what seemed like forever, for her baby's feet to heal, and not being able to do anything to help, made her more depressed than she has even been. She had hoped for more comfort for her baby, but instead she was suffering even more. Two weeks later, Marisa's feet were better, and she was scheduled to be transferred to the University Hospital, a more advanced medical institution on the neighboring Abyss Caye. However, on the advice of the Head Matron, the transfer was delayed for another week to allow more healing, thereby avoiding an embarrassing situation.

It was a bright sunny Monday after noon, and the local airplane climbed steadily higher and higher.

"Good afternoon ladies and gentlemen," a gentle masculine voice announced. "This is your pilot, Captain Norman Perkey, along with co-pilot Orlando Frost. Miss Bernadette Bolden and Miss Joylynn Prescod are your gracious hostesses for this flight."

"We are currently at an altitude of 2,000 feet and will level off at 18,000 feet. The weather is fair with a temperature of 79 degrees. The wind is calm and blowing north north-west. We should be landing in approximately three and a half hours.

Jolene and Marisa were now miles off the ground, and a long way from home. Marisa's little eyes looked pitifully up at her mother as if to say "Where are we? Where are we going?" She was obviously scared. Realizing this, Jolene held her close to her breast and encountered the strangest feeling of uneasiness she couldn't explain.

Jolene and Marisa arrived early in the evening on Abyss Caye's unsophisticated but interesting airport, having only two airplanes in good working condition that serviced the whole region. Its beautiful landscape was adorned with many tall palm tree branches, waiving in the sea breeze. Smaller palmate trees looking like ladies' hand-held fan with blades that opens and closes, enhanced with many kinds of shrubs, tropical flowers, and ferns, lined the entrance of the two-story terminal. Inside was a quaint little restaurant with the aroma of mouthwatering foods. An outdoor rest and dining area gaily decorated with bamboo furnishings, and an indoor rest area for weary travelers.

Hospitality was of the highest quality from friendly and courteous inhabitants and staff of the airlines. Jolene and Marisa were met by a paramedic party that transported them in a screaming ambulance to the University Hospital. Marisa seemed so scared and confused with all the commotion.

"I think she is frightened!" observed nurse Gilda Merchant in the paramedic party. "Let me hold her!"

Jolene passed Marisa over to the nurse who also kept her close to her breast.

The sound of a screaming ambulance indicates an emergency, and upon arriving at the Abyss Caye University Hospital, Jolene expected Marisa would have been attended to sometime that night, considering the severity of her case, but she was not. People came from far distances and waited overnight in the outpatient area for medical attention, if they survived the night.

Jolene and Marisa were escorted to the children's ward which was also crowded, and it seemed like they waited for approximately an hour and a half before one of the nurses settled Marisa in a crib.

"She'll be all right!" the nurse told Jolene. "You must leave her now. The doctor will see her tomorrow," she explained. Then she suggested Jolene take a taxi to the place she would call home for the time she was in the country. She had no idea how much time that would be. Would her baby be treated and live another month or more, or would she die? If she did live for another month or more, what would she, Jolene, have done to earn a living so she would be able to stay in the country with her baby? Marisa was in the care of completely different people. What happened there was anyone's guess.

Those questions didn't enter her mind, but what she did think about was the thought of the possibility of leaving her baby there in a strange place with strange people, and that made her very uncomfortable, but she didn't know what she could do otherwise. They called the shots. She was only a visitor seeking their help, so she complied grudgingly and left the hospital.

Outside the hospital gate were many cars waiting to transport passengers; the drivers all dressed in short sleeve cotton shirts, khaki shorts, sandals, and straw hats to protect their heads from the broiling sun. Vying for service revealed that they were operating a taxi service although the cars were not labeled "taxi.

"You need a taxi, Miss?" one asked.

"Can I take you somewhere Miss?" the other asked in unison.

"Yes!" Jolene said and handed a piece of paper containing the intended address to the one who approached her first. She got in the back seat of the car while the chauffeur took care of her baggage.

"Nice flight Miss ... Ah, what's your name?" he asked her boldly, striking up a conversation.

"Jolene, Jolene Tradis" she said.

"Pretty name Miss Jolene" he complemented. "I am Patrick".

"Yes! very nice flight!" she answered his question. Wish it were for a more pleasant reason though. I brought by baby for treatment at the University Hospital, hoping to take her home better than she came."

"We have good doctors and nurses here. With some faith and lots of love, you just might.

"Thanks! I need that word of courage".

In twenty-five minutes, the taxi chauffeur deposited her in front of a beautiful sea green painted bungalow, located at the edge of the city.

"This is the address," he said.

She paid and thanked him; walked halfway up the path of Mrs. Harvey's house and stopped to admire the well-kept garden in front of the house. She approached the front door, knocked timidly, and waited for it to open.

"Good night!" she said in a rather shy way to the gray hair, grandmotherly-looking lady who opened the door.

"I'm Jolene!" she introduced herself.

"Oh yes! come in, come in! I am Mother Harvey. My daughter-in-law told me to expect you. She went to get her hair fixed but promised to return soon. Have a seat."

Before Jolene was comfortably seated, Mother Harvey bombarded her with questions in an effort to entertain her.

"How was your flight over? How is the baby? Did you leave her at the hospital? She paused suddenly, realizing that she wasn't giving Jolene a chance to answer her questions.

"Yes! the baby is at the University Hospital. The nurse told me she wouldn't be seen by any doctor before tomorrow, so I should leave her and come on home. She isn't in the best shape, but I have faith she will make it through the night, and I'll see her tomorrow. Tough little thing that she is."

"That's good. It's good to have a lot of faith," Mother Harvey said trying to put her mind at ease.

"The flight was a pleasant one." Jolene said attempting to answer the remaining unanswered questions. "Flying for the first time, I had all kinds of doubts and fears, but I said a little prayer that renewed my faith and confidence".

"We boarded the local airplane at one o'clock, and very soon we were off the ground climbing higher and higher.

The pilot, co-pilot and flight attendants were all kind. They made us as comfortable as possible. The pilot had such a gentle masculine voice when he announced:

"Good afternoon ladies and gentlemen, this is Captain Norman Perkins, your pilot for this flight, along with co-pilot Orlando Frost. Miss Bernadette Bolden and Miss Joylynn Prescod are your gracious hostesses," then a slight pause as the intercom made a gurgling sound. "We are currently at an altitude of 2,000 feet and level off at 18,000 feet. The weather is fair with a temperature of 69 degrees. The wind is calm and blowing north north-west. We should be landing in approximately three and a half hours."

"So precise was his announcement" she added and was silent for a second trying to remember every minute of that first flight. "A few bumps kept us alert. The snack was just enough to fill our eye-tooth, but that is what a snack is. I enjoyed the flight. Wish it were for a more pleasurable reason though. Flying is quite an experience," she concluded.

"I've never been on an airplane, and as old as I am, I know I wouldn't be interested in such an adventure," Mother Harvey told her with certainty. "I don't trust those things."

"You're not old, and you probably would enjoy flying. Put a little faith in modernism," a female voice advised her gently.

Mother Harvey's daughter-in-law Patricia Harvey, known to Jolene only as Mrs. Harvey, had returned from the beauty parlor.

Remembering she needed to fill her pantry, she stopped at the grocery store to do some shopping. When she got home, she entered the house in the back door to the kitchen; store the groceries she bought on her way home, then went into the living room to join Jolene and Mother Harvey.

Jolene met Mrs. Harvey only twice a few years before, but through a friend who knew her for many years, she, Jolene was invited to stay at the Harvey's home while Marisa was in the hospital.

At the sight of her again, Jolene remembered the first time they met. "She is still thin; she keeps her figure very well. Her hair is so neatly done, and that dress fits like a glove," Jolene thought.

"Jolene?" Mrs. Harvey asked looking at her questionably, having met only twice before and not being quite sure."

"Yes!"

"It's good to see you again!"

Jolene rose and shook hands with her. "Have you been here long?"

"I've been here long enough to see a little bit of the city." Questions started rolling off Mrs. Harvey's tongue, but unlike

Mother Harvey's questioning, Jolene was allowed to answer them one at a time.

By the end of the preliminaries, they became better acquainted, and the reason for the visit to Abyss Caye was discussed.

"I assume you left the baby at the hospital. How was she when you took her there?" Mrs. Harvey asked.

"She wasn't the best, but I have faith she will be treated, and we'll be back home soon". Jolene said not thinking what she would do to keep her there.

"How is Bluehold Cove and my dear friend Lucas?"

"Bluehold Cove is changed, but Lucas is the same old Lucas, still trying to be a 'macho man' without teeth".

CHAPTER

8

On Abyss Caye, breakfast or tea alone was served in the morning, dinner was served at midday, and tea again in the evening. Mrs. Harvey prepared fresh home baked bread and fried fish for her guest Jolene, and baker's bread for Mother Harvey, because she was not able to eat fresh homemade bread in the night.

After a good meal, the group dispersed and regrouped in the living room to go over the day's events and other businesses; to make plans for the next day, then went to bed.

Approximately five and a half hours after arriving at Mrs. Harvey's home and settled in bed, there was a knock on the front door. Mrs. Harvey, Jolene's hostess, answered the door. From the bedroom she could hear voices, but the words were not clear, and since she was not a member of the household, but a visitor, it didn't interest her to see who it was. Regretfully after, she thought it would have been good if she did. She was just about to fall asleep when Mrs. Harvey came to her room, sat next to her on the bed and said: "That was the police. He came to tell you that your baby died."

Why didn't she call me to the door to talk with the police? Jolene wondered. Maybe because she wanted to break the news gently to me, telling me herself. She was asking and answering her own questions. She had been doing that a lot.

She cried and cried, but somehow, she felt she was crying because she was expected to cry, and not because of the loss. She really did not know what she was feeling. The reality of the announcement of Marisa's death did not register with her even though she expected it would come someday. It was as though she had just then entered the twilight zone consciously, with no idea of what was supposed to be done in the case of death. Never in her life did she have such an undertaking; she attended funerals; she was just only beginning to deal with life.

Being aware that Jolene did not possess the knowledge of conducting a funeral, especially in a foreign country, Mrs. Harvey kindly offered her help.

"Give me what money you have and the baby's bonnet to bury her in, and I'll prepare everything."

Jolene gave her most of what little money she had carried to live on, and the baby's bonnet.

Early the next morning, Mrs. Harvey took Jolene to the Registrar of births and deaths office on the south side of the city, so she can sign the death certificate and send a telegram to her mother Armenia Tradis, since she, Armenia, had become sympathetic and very fond of her beautiful first grandchild. Then Mrs. Harvey took Jolene back home and went about the rest of the day's business.

The burial was arranged for the end of that day, so Mrs. Harvey went home to pick up Jolene to attend. On her way to the burial, she stopped at an office that could have been her workplace and picked up two women and two men. Mrs. Harvey introduced them only as her friends then she led the two-car funeral procession; the ladies in her car followed by the men in the other car, carrying a tiny coffin.

They proceeded to what Jolene perceived to be a sparsely occupied cemetery and parked the cars a good distance from the spot that was the burial site.

Mrs. Harvey and the two men took the tiny coffin to the site under a tree. Jolene, in a somewhat disarrayed state of mind, and listless in body, having been through such an ordeal, watched and waited in the car, as they lowered it into the ground.

From experience she knew that it was customary for prayers to be said and hymns sang at the grave site. With lips of one of the men moving, that could have been the case then, but she couldn't be sure from the distance between them.

The ladies waited with Jolene in the car trying to comfort her. "That baby couldn't live, because she was too pretty," one lady said to Jolene. That was an 'Old Wives Tale' or a belief that if a baby was born with fairly nice features, he or she would not live; an obviously ridiculous superstition.

Marisa did look like a doll, but Jolene was surprised to hear her say that. She thought old wife's tales and strange beliefs were entertained only in her country, but after all they were islanders too.

The coffin was never opened to reveal its contents. Jolene was too distraught to be conscious of the situation. Every time she thought about the condition Marisa was in, she cringed, hence partly the reason she was reluctant to view the body if there was one, therefore she did not view the body before the burial of the tiny coffin. Jolene, being naive and trusting, wouldn't think anything other than her baby would be in it anyway.

When all was said and done, and she was able to concentrate, she realized that she didn't see her baby in the tiny coffin before it was put in the ground. Grief-stricken, she was not conscious enough to think that she should see her baby one last time. She knew however, that she had lost her forever and guilt stepped in.

"I didn't say goodbye to my baby. What kind of mother am I"? She moaned.

Mrs. Harvey tried to console her with the idea that she didn't do anything wrong. That the probability of it being better to remember her baby in life, rather than in death, although she wasn't sure whether Marisa was dead or alive, not having seen her in the coffin.

Either way life or death was haunting. The last she saw of her was the day they arrived at the hospital.

Jolene was not even asked to identify and claim the body for burial. How could Mrs. Harvey be sure which baby she was to bury, not having met her before? Jolene wondered. Well, there are records and information and the like. She was dancing to her own tune again, asking and answering her own questions.

After the funeral, Mrs. Harvey, thoughtful as she was, arranged a date for herself and a blind date for Jolene. They met the following afternoon and Mrs. Harvey made the introductions.

"This is my friend Bertram," she told Jolene, and to Bertram, "this is Jolene."

Bertram was apprised of the situation prior to the meeting, which was good, because Jolene was neither one for much talk, nor did she want to have to explain.

After the introduction Bertram said gently:

"I'm sorry to hear about your baby. Maybe there is something I can do to help you feel better."

"Thanks!" Jolene quickly replied.

"We can all take a nice long trip deep into the countryside where tourists frequent; do a little dancing to end the day.

That will take your mind off the death of the baby." That was Mrs. Harvey's antidote for an unpleasant situation. So, they did.

It was beautiful country. The season was summer with sweltering heat, but a light sea-breeze blew in contrast. The hills were green and adorned with beautiful flowers; numerous species of orchid seemed to grow everywhere, and flourishing ferns decked the foothills. The narrow-paved roads that led to the countryside, twisted, and turned through the hills more than a snake, casting some fear to Jolene's already frayed nerves, but experienced driving landed her there and back home safely. On the way out, Mrs. Harvey stopped to visit with her friends the Uhuru family, who owned a large white two-story home. She made introductions and they all got acquainted.

"Nice home!" Jolene complimented looking around the room.

"Nice people too! Mrs. Harvey told her complementing them also.

"Thanks! Mrs. Uhuru acknowledged their compliments.

"You know, he, referring to her friend Mr. Uhuru, is known as the 'Loa Spirits Guru' in these parts." Mrs. Harvey mentioned casually to Jolene in their conversation.

"I see!" Jolene replied with a forced smile and no real knowledge of what that was supposed to mean.

They chatted with the Uhurus a bit, said goodbye, and went to a night club or 'nightspot' as it was called in Abyss Caye.

Dining and dancing could not make Jolene forget, but it did help for the minute. The food was very tasty and the music inviting to the feet. The company she could have done without. Blind date or any date was not appropriate to her.

The trip back home seemed like forever. They drove over hills, around curves, across bridges to get back home. Tired and frustrated Jolene sat silently for the duration of the trip. She just wanted to be left alone with her thoughts.

On the fourth day of her stay, Jolene ventured out to do some shopping for a few souvenirs with what little money she had left.

"If you're taking the bus, be careful. Keep your bag closed. It can be brutal out there," Mother Harvey shouted in her native accent, from the kitchen window.

"Is that so?" Jolene shouted back.

"Oh yes, that's so! Mother Harvey assured her. Jolene thanked her kindly and left the house. The buses were crowded alright; people were everywhere, even hanging on the outside. Many passengers transported their market goods by bus. Chickens were most present. I suppose in that case you could lose just about anything, Jolene thought. Her beloved grandfather Papa John used to say jokingly, that some people in that part of the world could steal the sugar from the sweet buns they make.

She made it back home without anything missing. Mother Harvey met her at the door with the greeting, "just in time for dinner".

"Oh! that's what I smelt from two blocks away? Jolene teased.

"Oh yes child. I make only the best for my visitors."

Mother Harvey had prepared a delicious local dish of seasoned rice and stuffed baked red snapper, large enough to feed an army, drenched in a sauce made with locally grown herbs and spices, and steamed vegetables.

"How did your shopping go," she enquired as they sat down to eat dinner.

"It went very well. I'm amazed at what I bought with the little money I had."

They exchanged ideas in shopping till dinner was over, then it was time to start packing; it was time to return home to her country.

Amid her packing, Mrs. Harvey asked Jolene if she would give her all the baby's clothes for a friend who was expecting a baby.

That was odd Jolene thought, because they were not receiving clothes and blankets. Marisa was seven months old, and Jolene had made her clothes to her size. Most of it being pink, the choice color for girls. There was one special little red and white polka-dot dress she made as Marisa's traveling outfit, that she never wore, since she was taken from the hospital directly to the airport in a hospital gown. Jolene would have liked the pleasure of taking Marisa's picture wearing that dress. Moreover, who knew what the sex of Mrs. Harvey's friend's baby would be? It probably wouldn't make any difference as long as he or she had clothes to wear.

The polka-dot dress was Jolene's favorite piece. Whenever she saw a red and white polka-dot dress in the stores, or in the streets, or anywhere, she would have flashbacks of the dress she made for Marisa that she had a hard time parting with.

What would I have done with her clothes? She asked herself. The idea of another baby was farfetched, and who knew what kind of baby it would be anyway, she reminded herself. Moreover, the clothes would not be small enough for a newborn baby, so she gave all of Marisa's clothes to Mrs. Harvey for her friend. Marisa's only remaining possession was 'Teddy,' her Steiff bear since it did not accompany them on the trip, he was left behind and later given to Marisa's cousin Estella.

CHAPTER

9

Jolene's flight was scheduled for mid-morning after all the businesses were done. With her bags packed she said goodbye to Mother Harvey, then it was time to leave. She was leaving without her baby dead or alive, not even a scrap of clothes. She didn't have a death certificate; no burial plot information; no autopsy report indicating cause of death; no proof whatsoever of her existence or non-existence. She never felt so empty; so empty and very much alone. Ignorance and stress was the reason for the lack of those documents.

Unbelievable as it may seem, thoughts of documents of any kind were not uppermost in her mind. She did not think that those documents were supposed to be issued to her, and at the time she couldn't care less. Nine months pregnancy and seven months misery and mothering which ended in total lost had drained her mentally and physically.

Before leaving for the airport, Mrs. Harvey took Jolene to the University College to see Steve, one of Marisa's uncles that was pursuing a degree in Business. He had never met Jolene and Marisa, being away from home for many years, but was aware of their existence. He was obviously saddened by the death of his niece, but more because he did not know her, missing a piece of the family puzzle.

"I'm sorry. I would have been there for you at the burial had I known about it" Steve told Jolene.

"One good thing is that you're still young," he said trying to comfort her, "still of child-bearing age. You can have more Sweetie-Sweeties" that was the 'pet' name Jolene told him, was given to Marisa by her paternal grandmother Beryl, Lindsy's and Steve's mother. Then like the nurses at the hospital back home, he added teasingly: "Go home and get started on another one. I'm sure you'll have better luck this time."

"I hardly think that to be an immediate possibility," Jolene said sheepishly, "since your brother and I are not on our best behavior."

"I'm sorry." He said apologetically. "I didn't know it had come to that. Well, I hope you can resolve your differences and get on with your lives together."

"Thanks Steve. I wish you God's speed with your studies." she told him.

"Thank you. The family will ask about me, I'm sure. Be sure to say that I'm doing just fine." Steve admonished her jokingly.

"I'm sorry to have to run off; you must excuse me I have to leave now before I miss my flight."

"Hope you have a safe trip home; the weather isn't exactly summery anymore."

Steve was right. The weather had changed to be more like fall. The sky looked like somebody had taken a giant brush and smeared mud all over it. The weather report did call for rain. The stormy season created such unpredictable weather.

I'm sorry you didn't see Steve earlier he would have been a good comfort to you" Mrs. Harvey told Jolene. She took Jolene to the airport. Jolene thanked her and asked her to convey her gratitude to Mother Harvey and all the other kind people who helped her in any way. Said goodbye and boarded the plane.

It took approximately three and a half hours back to Bluehole Cove and Jolene was back on familiar ground. It seemed like she had just gone to a nearby town for four days and came back. Living was the same as she had left it, so there was no problem falling into the old routine before Marisa's stay in the hospital. Life goes on. Grieving was not on her agenda.

Lindsy was the only one in the group who appeared to be concerned as Jolene briefly mentioned the events on Abyss Caye. He listened intently to all that Jolene had to say; how she didn't see Marisa in the coffin that Mrs. Harvey's friend deposited in the grave, therefore she didn't know if Marisa really died and was buried that day; the fact that she wasn't directly contacted by the police who delivered the message of the death to the house where she was staying, informing her hostess, Mrs. Harvey, who then relayed the news to her. She didn't talk with a doctor at the university hospital and didn't remember being asked about doing an autopsy which apparently, according to the death certificate, was performed. There was so much more information to reveal but Jolene was not in the mood to do so.

Lindsy told his mother of Marisa's death without any explanation of the cause. She apologized for her unbecoming behavior and condoled with him and Jolene.

Neither Jolene's family nor friends enquired about her time spent there, and Jolene told them only a brief summary, therefore no one knew exactly what transpired in those four days on that Caye. She figured the reason they didn't asked was because they did not want to remind her any more than she wanted to be reminded, although for years at Christmas time, she could smell the odor of the Bluehole Cove Children's hospital where Marisa spent most of her short life. She couldn't get away from her thoughts.

Her job as Secretary to a Puisne Judge was filled by a temporary replacement until she returned, so she went back to work, but total concentration wasn't as easy as she had anticipated. Her mind oftentimes strayed to Marisa. How happy she was before the progression of her illness. Tickle or talk to she would laugh or smile a beautiful smile. How pretty she looked when she was dressed up and seemed to know she was about to go somewhere, with 'Brownie' bear, her companion, close to her in her prom.

Jolene could still hear her faint cry; feel her warm, frail, tender little body next to her bosom, and that made her heartbeat faster and her eyes misty, and she would quickly remind herself of her oath not to brood and start healing. She was determined to be whole again and take things in stride; take a trip somewhere; see different things and different people as good mental healing therapy.

At work her co-workers would sometimes ask about her stay on Abyss Caye and she would feel obliged to tell them. She would relate some of the sad events that ended with emptiness. Then to lighten the somber mood she tells them about the day Marisa was born; how she begged the nurse to take her anywhere to ease the contraction pain.

"Please nurse, please take me" I told her.

"Take you where child, take you where?" the nurse she asked me. "Take me anywhere, I don't care, as long as this pain stops." They all laughed and made comments mocking me.

"We mi tink yo dah moh woman, Ruth my little sister told me" meaning "We thought you were more woman or braver woman."

"Now yo wah noh how barley grow" was my Aunt Agata's comment, meaning that it is like knowing what it's like to have and care for a baby. She tells them about the day Marisa was christened, and the small pink chamber pot gift from Bernie, one of her Godmothers to start her potty training.

Capering around the office, she showed how Lindsy took the little chamber pot and capered around the yard, telling his friends to put money in it if they didn't bring a present. Good friends as they were, everyone emptied his pocket of change in the pot, or a dollar or two from their wallet, telling Lindsy that he just wanted to get "filthy rich". In his intoxicated state he attempted to dance on top of the tables, from one to another with the pot of money in hand, he missed and fell in the tub of ice blocks and water. That sobered him up some.

Showing her co-workers men and women how he did - not on the table of course; she fell off her spike heel shoes unto the floor, just as her boss walked in the door; her dress thrown over her head and everything underneath was on display. One of the ladies tried to hurriedly cover her up, and she fell on top of Jolene giving everyone including the boss,

a good view of her display. Jolene was so embarrassed, but laughed along with the rest, lightening the somber mood, she created with the sad story.

"That was so funny, so funny." A good laugh would always be regarded as a part of healing therapy for Jolene.

With Marisa gone Jolene agreed to pick up the pieces of her severed relationship with Lindsy, with hopes that life with him would be better. They dated often for a while, doing all the things they used to do together; travelling, dining, and dancing, going to the horse races, the movies and many other activities which included taking Jolene to visit his family. It seemed like he was prepared to make a commitment to her then.

Unfortunately, within the time they were apart, Lindsy was being friendly with other women. He became decadent, and coquetry was now first and foremost in his life, and his attention to Jolene waned once again.

Jolene realizing there were no ties to bind them having lost Marisa, forgave him and made good riddance of him.

CHAPTER

10

Still in a state of vulnerability after two or three years, Jolene attended different functions at which suitors were always ready to solicit her affection; that made her feel appreciated.

The annual Festival of Arts which included arts and crafts, singing groups and choirs, solos, poetry, dance, piano recitals, and drama, was a function held at the Jubilee Art Center, located on the foreshore of Bluehole Cove city, attended by performers, dignitaries, and the public.

Jolene arrived with Aunt Agata who had been a participant for twelve years, reciting what seemed like endless poems, but non-the-less applauded by the audiences. Her memory was quite remarkable for an eighty-year-old woman.

Included in the program, is a fifteen-minute intermission, at which time some audience would go outside the building to stretch their legs, or smoke; get acquainted with other attendees or did whatever felt good to do.

Jolene decided she wanted a breath of fresh air and left the building while Aunt Agata made acquaintances with whoever was willing to listen after her long-winded poetry; walked a few feet towards the sea wall and stood gazing at the moon in all its splendor; its light glowing brightly on the rippling waters; sailing sloops passing in the distance. A light sea breeze blowing her hair caressing her slightly rounded face.

"Beautiful night isn't it, Jolene?" a soft, tender masculine voice addressed her from behind, startling her a bit. She turned and was face to face with that masculine voice, she heard.

"Oh! I'm sorry! I didn't mean to startle you!" Joel apologized.

"Oh yes! Yes! It is a beautiful night," she stuttered.

"Don't you just love the moon when it's so beautiful? "Enhancing your face, the way it does, sends my pulse racing," he told her extending his hand to her.

"My name is Joel - Joel Jennings."

"Good to meet you," she told him, shaking his hand timidly, "but how do you know my name?"

"I saw you go into the center accompanied by Mrs. Mansfield my dear friend, and my heart and I agreed that I should find out who you are. So, I sought Mrs. Mansfield, and she was kind enough to inform me that you are her niece, and to increase my luck, here you are looking radiant in the moonlight".

They exchanged small talk about themselves, and by the end of the intermission, became acquainted enough to agree on seeing each other again.

"Have you made plans for Thanksgiving Day?" Jolene asked him. "No! I think I'll hibernate like a bear."

"How dull!" Jolene told him.

Come over to my house, I'm fixing dinner!"

Thanksgiving was the following week. He was happy to be invited for dinner prepared by her dainty little hands.

Joel Jennings, a handsome, well-groomed, mild-mannered retired Air Force Officer, was the son of the locally famous artist Eli Jennings. His tour of duties in the Middle East had concluded, having been placed on permanent disability, because of an injury he sustained to his pancreas in a military confrontation, causing him to become diabetic. This bit of medical history he felt would be harmful to a relationship, if ever there was one, therefore he thought it unwise to reveal the whole story to Jolene in the course of getting acquainted for fear of rejection and did a good job of concealing it. Jolene also did not find it necessary to immediately reveal details of events with Marisa.

Joel's attention increased and his affections grew deeper. Besieged by all this; believing that this time she would be happy unto death, Jolene unwittingly reciprocated and created a friendship. For a year, every day was like Valentine's Day. Joel showered her with flowers, chocolates and balloons, cards with beautiful sentimental words; the friendship escalated to a relationship.

When the actual Valentine's Day arrived, and Joel, now quite comfortable with the situation, decided it was time to ask Jolene to marry him. Jolene too, had thoughts concerning the result of their friendship. To celebrate the day, she invited Joel over for a romantic evening of dinner and dancing at her home. She was preparing his favorite Lobster with a spicy seafood sauce and steamed vegetables. Coconut tarts and Custard Apple ice cream were the desserts. During the preparation, her telephone rang.

"Could I entice you to accompany me this evening?" Joel asked. "We can get all formal and go to the Seawinds Ballroom for dinner and do a little dancing."

"What's the occasion?" Jolene asked him.

"You see, my heart tells me I should talk to your heart, and I thought Seawinds would be the ideal setting for a heart-to-heart."

"It seems to me your heart does a lot of talking."

"Oh yes! but only to angels" Joel admitted.

"What does your heart want you to talk to my heart about?"

"I'm sworn to secrecy until we meet."

"Well then, you certainly could. I'm enticed. It's always a pleasure to dine with you." She conveniently forgot to mention that she was in the midst of preparing them a romantic evening. She thought getting all dressed up, and going out on the town dining and dancing, might be just what the doctor ordered.

"Eight o'clock, my dear?" Joel asked.

"Eight o'clock it is, sir" she repeated.

Like most women do when preparing for a romantic evening, Jolene went to her clothes closet and selected one dress after another, trying to determine which would best suit the occasion. Time running short, she selected a beautiful crimson A-line polyester, off shoulder dress, accessorized with a single strand of freshwater black pearls and earrings, designed by jewelers on the island. Three-inches high heels black suede shoes that elevated her close to Joel's height, and bag to match. She didn't have time to go to the hairdresser, so she quickly twisted her hair in a bun in the back of her head, dressed it with a crimson rose, and she was all ready and raring to go.

Joel arrived at her home promptly at Eight o'clock, disciplined as he was, being a military retiree, his attire fit to meet the king; black three-piece suite, white shirt, a crimson bow tie and handkerchief and Alfani men's black shoes. He didn't give her flowers because he had much more in mind and in his pocket for that night.

On arrival at the Seawinds Ballroom, Joel and Jolene were seated without hesitation, in the exclusive dining area Joel had reserved; sparsely lit, and sparsely occupied, not far from the beverage bar, creating a very cozy atmosphere.

A young waitress neatly dressed in a modest, but attractive Sea Breeze Teal outfit, outlining her slim body, served them Jolene's favorite red wine, while the local orchestra played her favorite song "Red Wine Entwines Your Heart with Mine" requested by Joel.

"Care to dance?"

"Yes! I certainly care to dance to my favorite song, if the wine hasn't gone straight to my head, because if it did, I'll be falling all over you.

It felt so good, so right having her in his arms. This must be the right time to broach the subject he thought. For them both, life was good. However, the dance ended on a rather sour note.

With the anxiety of the main purpose of the evening, Joel had forgotten to take his medication and the sugar in his blood was depleted.

He became uncontrollable acting like he was drunk. Jolene, ignorant of his medical history, thought the red wine went to his head, rather than his heart like the song said. She thought he was drunk, when in fact he was experiencing insulin shock - something Jolene knew nothing about but was soon enlightened by one of the waitresses familiar with his condition, being diabetic herself.

"I'll get him something with sugar to drink," she said. "As soon as the sugar gets into his bloodstream, he'll be fine. Getting him to drink might be a task. I'm glad that he isn't out in the street somewhere, because he could be mistaken for a drunk and be arrested."

"That's what I thought" Jolene said. "I thought he was drunk." "It's a condition that is easily mistaken for drunkenness," the waitress went on telling her.

She was so right about getting him to drink. Being in a somewhat incoherent state, it took them some time to get him to cooperate, but they did. He gulped down the drink and in a short time, he was fine.

Embarrassed by this unfortunate incident, Joel knew he owed Jolene an explanation.

"You have been very good to me and for me," he told her, then paused for a moment. "I apologize for that incident. He paused again trying to think the right words to say. Jolene's curious eyes stayed on him as he spoke.

"I owe you an explanation of the reason for my military retirement," he continued realizing that if she agrees to marry him, he will have to reveal his well-kept medical secret. He would have to tell someday anyhow, so he did.

Steering silently deep into the glass of wine, trying to find a starting point to his story, he cleared his throat massaging his glass.

"Penny for your thoughts" Jolene interrupted.

Joel looked up at her. "My thoughts are worth a whole lot more than penny, and they are all wrapped up in my explanation to you about my military retirement" he told her.

In my Military Officer's capacity, I was deployed to engage in a military conflict years ago. Traveling from one outfit to another to inspect the troops, my accompanying officers and I were ambushed, and I took a bullet in my chest injuring my pancreas, causing it to stop producing enough insulin my body needs, therefore my blood sugar gets too low sometimes and causes diabetic shock. In that state I am incoherent and uncontrollable until I get some sugar in my blood. I try to be careful to take insulin injection and have sugar of some sort at hand always.

Jolene sat silently looking at him sympathetically.

She reached for his hand and held it saying – "I didn't have any knowledge of such a medical condition. It must be burdensome to live with" she said caringly.

"Hard to begin with, but eventually it becomes your life. It is not an easy road to travel for you or a caregiver; it takes love, patience, and real caring.

With a sigh of relief Joel, unburdened of that secret part of his life, took the glass to his head and sipped the wine deep in thought of Hannah, his other well-kept secret.

He will have to tell her about Hannah his first wife also, who after three years of marriage, was not willing to honor the promise of 'in sickness or in health' anymore, so to the best of his knowledge, he explained that part of his life too.

"You know Jolene" he said, "for me military life was very lonely at times, not having a family to go home to when I left the base. With not much time for a social life, I literally stayed on the base most of the time, but I met and married a young woman, Hannah, who promised to be my best friend and caregiver for life. We were happy; we were blessed with many material things; life was good at the start. Then my pancreas got worse and diabetic shocks were more frequent. Hannah decided she couldn't help me anymore and walked away from the marriage." His explanation was plain and simple.

"Well, like you said, it takes love, patience and caring" and not everyone has that capacity to love and care that much and has the patience of Job too" Jolene reminded him.

"I totally agree my dear" Joel agreed.

The food was served, but the mood of the evening was changed. They both looked at it with disdain not eating; they lost their raving romantic appetite. Neither one of them was hungry anymore. Moreover, Joel was bothered by indecision of broaching the subject of marriage to Jolene, fearing the worse. Tension was mediocre, but Jolene was determined for them to have fun, despite all odds.

"I believe this food was put here for us to eat don't you" she said jokingly.

"I do believe" he answered, and both turned on their appetite vowing to enjoy it.

"Next to your delightful company, the food is just great" she managed to say convincingly.

"Thank you! You're such an angel," he whispered, kissing her, putting them back in a romantic mood.

Reaching into his coat pocket he retrieved a small box neatly wrapped in colorful paper and sealed with a tiny gold-colored paper heart.

"I would really like to have the pleasure of being married to an angel". I cannot get down on my knees, but if you could accept a standing proposal; he placed the small box in her hand.

"Will you marry me?"

Jolene's face lit up. Is this the result she had in mind? It must have been, because without hesitation she replied.

"I can't see a halo above my head, but yes! I'll marry you."

Jolene took the little box from Joel, removed the ring, and allowed Joel to place it on her finger. She was officially engaged to be married to Joel.

When they met at the Arts Center that night, birthdays were one of the topics of conversation and Joel's birthday was now two weeks away from their blissful engagement night.

"This calls for a little celebration to tell everybody" she told Joel, and he agreed wholeheartedly. Invitations went out to family and friends as a surprise party for Joel's birthday.

The celebration was held on the weekend of Joel's birthday at the Seawinds Ballroom where their hearts talked to each other and agreed to a relationship two weeks before. All the invited guests attended and Joel, thinking that they would surprise the guests with the announcement of their engagement, was surprised himself to find it was his birthday party as well. With the celebration in full swing Jolene quieted the guests so she could make her announcement.

"Is everyone having a good time?" she called out.

"Couldn't be better!" was one reply with everybody in agreement. "We, Joel and I appreciate your presence and decided to reward you with our announcement of, she hesitated then together they said, "our engagement!"

Congratulations came from everyone shaking hands, kissing, and hugging with delight, expecting to be on the guests list for the wedding.

CHAPTER

11

The Jennings being people of grandeur, planned for a quiet but impressive wedding in early autumn which seemed to be in a hurry to arrive, to be held at the Art Gallery, owned by Joel's father Eli Jennings, rather than the church they attended.

At the Gallery professional decorators did an exquisite job decorating in grand style, with exotic accent of different orchids and ferns among other decorations. Invited relatives and close friends attended in formal attire looking most elegant.

Jolene's full length, ivory lace dress with a sweet-heart neckline, bordered with little daisies, caressed her well rounded youthful body; long sleeves accessorized with cultured pearl buttons. In her elegantly styled hair, she wore a small tiara with a short white veil attached. A pair of ivory lace with pearl beads shoes to match her dress. As tradition: something old-a white handkerchief embroidered with blue orchids. For something new-a single strand of cultured pearls. Something borrowed: a pair of cultured pearl earrings; all created by the people of Bluehole Cove; and blue, orchids in her bridal bouquet. The traditional men's formal black suit and vest, white shirt, blue bowtie and handkerchief, a blue orchid on his lapel and black shoes.

Officiating was Jolene's boss Puisne Judge Isaac Warding, dressed in gown and wig to perform the ceremony with words of marital wisdom.

At the end he gave them a word of advice for the times when it seemed like they were slowly drifting apart. He said:

"Marriage is such a blessed and blissful institution, but there will be times when it seems like the bliss is disappearing and being replaced with careless; you can't care less. Things are not what they used to be; the honeymoon is over before it got started with the next phase looking forward to having a family.

When you start experiencing that time, try to remember these words by one with some experience.

TO SOON AFTER THE HONEYMOON

Remember When? What Happened?
Remember when we met and we just knew
    we LOVED each other?
Remember when we wed, we vowed to
    never LOVE ANOTHER?
Remember when we said that we would
    always LEND A HAND
With chores, with children and
    the like whatever else we can?
      WHAT HAPPENED?

Remember when we promised
    we would CURTAIL EXPENSES?
Remember when we used to come
    to each other's DEFENSES?
Remember when we said that we'd
    be FRIENDS, that we'd be EQUAL?
That we would show RESPECT and would
    not be too DICTATORIAL?
      WHAT HAPPENED?

Remember when we LAUGHED
    at silly things we said or did?
Remember how we CRIED or FROWNED
    at things that GOD forbid?
Remember we agreed if we FORGIVE
    that we'd be wise
And when we disagreed on things
    that we would COMPROMISE?
      WHAT HAPPENED?

Remember when we went to church
We PRAYED for what we heard?
Remember when our faith was
    strong and ACTED on his word?
Remember how we planned a life
    filled with much hopes and dreams?
We planned for HONESTY
    and TRUTH and not what it now seems?
      WHAT HAPPENED?

DO YOU REMEMBER WHEN IT HAPPENED?

Let's remember our promises and vows
Let's strive to keep them all
I've heard it said so many times
And read it in GOD's Word that
Pride goes before destruction
And a haughty spirit before a fall

LET'S NOT DESTROY THEM ALL

After offering such advice of remembrance, he disrobed and joined
the guests in the celebrations. Offering the blessing was the young
Reverend Daniel Lians, not yet licensed to perform marriages, also

dressed in his official clergy attire. Miss Carol Kandy gave a rendition of the ever-popular love song: "Love of An Angel" accompanied by a seven-piece orchestra which provided the music for the occasion; beautifully done. The "I Dos" were said, and the mood was set for dancing.

During his stay in the Middle East, Joel became well acquainted with people of different backgrounds, and professions, including belly dancers. At the Evening Star night club where he spent a little of his free time, getting acquainted with the patrons and staff including the dancing girls, he was especially friendly with Naida, who was the lead dancer at the club. She was an interesting young lady with an adventurous mind. She planned to leave home to explore other parts of the world someday. Joel had boasted to her about his enchanting homeland Bluehole Cove, and she promised that she would one day go there to experience what it's like to be in Joel's paradise.

It had been many years since they met and became good friends, enjoying each other's company exploring many places of interest, learning their culture and language.

Remembering Naida's promise of visiting him and knowing that most people on Bluehole Cove island has only heard of belly dancing, Joel sent her a 'straight to the point' invitation to attend the wedding, with a request to perform her native dance, with hopes that it would be received by the conservative guests as just another culture. The invitation read:

> *You are cordially invited to witness the marriage of*
> *Joel Jennings and Jolene Tradis*
> *on Saturday September 10, 1990 at 3:00 pm*
> *to be held at the Eli Jennings Art Gallery*
>
> *P.S. You are welcomed to bring a guest. I would appreciate*
> *if you would perform your native dance for us.*

Naida did not have any special reason to visit Bluehole Cove other than seeing Joel again, and experience the charms of the island, therefore she had forgotten her promise to Joel to visit, and she did not have any interest anymore. However, when she received the invitation, her interest was rekindled and she, along with her dance accompanist arrived on Bluehole Cove island in time for the wedding.

Before the dancing began, Eli Jennings, Joel's father, introduced the happy married couple to the guests. Then congratulatory speeches were made by a few friends and relatives. After all the speeches were made, Joel introduced Naida with hopes of positive responses, then declaring the dance floor open.

"Fiends and relative," he called out. "I have a special entertainer to entertain you" he announced. "During my stay in the Middle East, I made friends with quite a few people and invited one friend and relatives to celebrate with us." He paused for a moment as everybody looked curiously at each other smirking and whispering.

"Yes! she accepted my invitation and is here with us," he finished his sentence.

"We have all heard of belly dancing I think, but I don't think that many have actually seen the dance. The ladies who perform this dance are called Belly Dancers.

Emerging from an adjoining room, Naida made her appearance dressed in her native dance attire; a decorated brassiere, beautiful assorted, beads around her neck, tiny tinkling bells on her hands; a full-length skirt fitting from her hips to her ankles, and lots of beautiful assorted, beads around her waist; head decorations all ablaze with colors and bare feet. A long shawl draped from her head partially covering her face.

"This is my friend Naida, she came all the way from a beautiful little village called Tyrini in the Middle East. The inhabitants there display very warm and unspoiled beauty inside and out.

"See, I keep promise to come visits you at your home. I also brought my musician Darius to help me" Naida told Joel. His attire was an oversize white long sleeve shirt, with many beads around his neck, and a colorful sash around his waist; on his head he wore a white turban with beads; all gaily decorated, but bare feet.

"You certainly did, and we're happy to have you both. Thank you for coming, we'll try to make your stay a good one." Joel assured them.

"You will dance for us now - won't you Naida?

"Yes!" she said smiling. "I dance for you!" Darius played an instrument that looked like a bagpipe, with attachments that played different instrument sounds, while Naida still smiling, danced tinkling her bells and twisting her body left and right, just enough to give the guests an idea of what belly dancing is. Joel had told her earlier how conservative the guests were but believed they would appreciate to learn something of other countries and their cultures.

The bride and guests were surprised all right. The dance was not what they had envisioned, but realized that it was cultural, and enjoyed it, nonetheless. They complimented Joel for the enlightening choice of entertainment, and Joel was pleased with their response.

However, Mrs. Armenia Tradis, Jolene's mother, was very disappointed in Joel's choice of entertainment, but felt constrained to voice her opinion of, 'somebody should call the police and have her arrested' like she said about the girls in the parade, and those at the beach wearing skimpy outfits. Everyone was having a good time, eating, drinking and merrymaking late into the night. The bride and groom said goodbye to their guests and left to spend some quiet time together, in a little cottage in the country, leaving Naida and Darius as guests to Joel's father.

Jolene was not exactly a model; however, she was enough for Joel to carry over the threshold. Joel gently took her in his arms, stepped over the threshold and kissed her the way he did the night he proposed.

The little cottage was certainly not a penthouse, but with the romantic mood still intact, they made themselves comfortable. They were legally and spiritually prepared to further their commitment and therefore consummated the marriage to last the rest of their lives.

Since a honeymoon was not in immediate plans, Joel and Jolene made good their promise of showing off their country to Naida and Darius, taking them to enjoy cruising to other islands on one of Bluehole

Cove's finest yachts, owned by Eli Jennings, Joel's father. Joel and Jolene took them to the best restaurant on the island and introduced them to different sea foods, island music and dance entertainments. They enjoyed immensely every minute of their stay.

Realizing the already short time they could stay on the island was depleted, Naida and Darius thanked their host and hostess kindly and hurriedly returned to Tyrini.

Married life for Joel and Jolene got off to a good start. Things were somewhat back to normal. Jolene now had something more to keep her mind occupied. She vowed to keep Joel's medical condition in control, so grieving for Marisa became much less. She remembered that her thoughts were that things would change with time. Well, things did change.

CHAPTER

12

Jolene's body suddenly started to feel like it did when she was expecting Marisa, three years previously; her heart skipped a beat or two.

No! Could it? Could it be that she unconsciously took Steve's and the nurse's advice of having another baby?

She became curious, but it was more than curiosity that sent her to see her doctor - it was 'scaryosity.' She was scared that she might have bad experiences like she did with Marisa, and she reflected on those experiences.

Remembering that the doctor had told her the disease Cystic Fibrosis was caused by the two parents having the same recessive gene, she wondered if it would happen again. Was she really expecting another baby? She certainly was. Number two baby was making its presence known.

She was happily married, but should she be happy about having another baby? Or was it too soon to try to forget the loss of the first.

Who was to be the authority on that? Maybe she should let the chips fall where they may, she thought.

Plans for a visit to her girlfriend Bernadine Briskett in the United States had been arranged long before the wedding, and she decided with

Joel's agreement to stay the course with that plan and took off again with the uncertainty of a pregnancy.

It felt good to be away from Bluehole Cove under better circumstances. Jolene was really beginning to unwind, relaxed, and looking forward to weekends; to have some fun shopping, partying, attending weddings, christenings, showers, picnics; any event her friend Bernadine was invited to, she was always welcomed to go along, and Bernadine was always being invited to functions.

Unfortunately, and all too soon, she was suddenly called by nature, and had to cease her comings and goings to attend. There certainly was a baby that was having some problems, which obviously caused Jolene to have some problems too.

Five months along, Jolene awoke one morning with a Terrible headache and was unable to get out of bed.

She had to depend on Bernadine for assistance. Gently raising herself from the bed, she tried not to rekindle the severity of the headache, stood up onto the floor, and was surprised by a stream of fluid.

Concern gripped her, having had the experience before, and she decided to visit a doctor. He assured her that there wasn't anything to be alarmed about. It was not false labor. However, home sounded like the place to be with problems, should anything else occur. So, she went tripping back to Bluehole Cove to await the arrival of her second child. Since she was still a few months away from the delivery date, and just hanging around would not hasten the time, she decided to go back to work; a job that would be convenient in her condition; something that would help to ease the boredom in waiting, as well as improving her financial situation, while Joel play housewife for a while.

Jolene went about her business day after day, feeling fit as a fiddle. She felt so good throughout the remaining months, she worked right up to the last weekend before delivery, against her husband's wishes.

Delivery by qualified Midwives was a common practice on Bluehole Cove island. Many women preferred birthing in that fashion rather than in a hospital knowing that it's a perfectly safe procedure, as long as the woman is kept under a doctor's care. They enjoy the comfort and privacy of a nursing home or their own home. Jolene made her choice to deliver at home. This time Nurse Robertson and her well-kept nursing home was unavailable; therefore, Nurse Carterby was retained to deliver the baby at Jolene's home.

Nagging backache started to develop, and this indicated to Jolene that it was now time to leave the job, and she did. With more time on her hands, she can now add the finishing touch to the preparation.

The layette she made was checked again for completeness. Jolene found herself wishing she had kept some of Marisa's belongings instead of giving away everything. Instinctively, her mother Armenia had advised her to keep some of Marisa's things.

"Save somethings, you might well need them again someday," her mother had said.

"Well, she was right. This is someday" she said to herself, "and I could use some of those things, but they are long gone. Why cry over spilt milk when I'll need those tears to - -." Jolene stopped as the first pain gripped her. Again, the long-awaited day had come.

Nurse Carterby was summoned late in the evening. When she arrived at Jolene's home, she had ample time to make the necessary preparations. Jolene's mother Armenia Tradis was very much in favor of this pregnancy, because this time Jolene was enjoying the sanctity of marriage. She therefore made herself available to assist with the delivery. Unlike Lyndsy, Joel was present to receive his first born, and never left Jolene's side. Like many first-time fathers he paced the floor and doing what he could to make her comfortable, fussing nervously all the way through the birthing.

Jolene appreciated his dedication but silently wished he would save some for the parenting journey ahead.

The contractions became stronger, and once again Jolene found herself rocking from side to side like an old cranky dory in a storm, pacing back and forth hoping for early relief.

Nurse Carterby performed a pelvic examination and concluded that the little person inside would be on time to go to mass at five o'clock in the morning. Midwives had a way of attaining a fairly good degree of accuracy with their predictions.

Sunday morning five o'clock the neighborhood Catholic Church bell rang out, calling saints and sinners alike to attend mass. Jolene meanwhile was calling for a drug of any kind to ease the pain of childbirth, just like she did once before, but like Nurse Robertson, Nurse Carterby was not one to administer drugs, and kept massaging and instructing, as the shoulders of the baby could not pass easily. Occasionally she would say a silent prayer for help, while Jolene labored on until it was over.

"It's a boy! and he's right in time to go to early morning mass," "Seven pounds one ounce" Nurse Carterby announced joyfully, a job well done by everybody.

"Everything seemed to be fine. Joel was now even more nervous, fussing over them ridiculously. The windows had to be shut tight; the drapes closed; the lights dimmed; the room quiet; and everyone visiting had to wear a mask.

"We'll call him Marlon Joel, Jolene whispered to Joel through spasms of after birth pains; he readily agreed.

Jolene watched his growth day by day and prayed that he would be healthy and strong. She thanked God for him every day. Caring for him left little time for the pain of the first, but never out of mind.

Three years of less pain from the first childbirth, but all the memories lingered on.

Joel, all puffed-up being 'daddy' thought it quite an achievement in his life considering his medical condition. He had a son to carry on his name – a father's ambition you know. Another of his ambitions was the love of airplanes; built many large-scale models and flew them at the annual air shows. Jolene usually accompanied him and helped in any way she could, with Marlon at her side, being the go-for boy, while she kept a watchful eye on them both. She was always willing to accepted the responsibility, but sometimes would rather be shopping or going to see a movie with her girlfriends.

Marlon at three-years-old, thought it no evil to feel like equal partner with his father; following in his footsteps; trying to build model airplanes with his guidance. Joel was really a mentor to him.

"We are buddies huh daddy?" he told Joel.

"Yes! We are buddies but I'm also your dad."

"Then you can spank me huh?"

"If it's necessary I can."

"I thought you love me daddy."

"I do love you, that is why I can spank you."

"I love you too daddy" he said climbing on Joel's lap, "but I won't spank you" he said with a bear hug.

"And you're my big boy" Jolene added.

"You can spank me too?"

"Yes! but not if you be a good boy." she told him.

"Then you don't love me mommy?"

"Ooh Yes! I love you very much because you are my big boy."

"I love you too" he told her with a big slobbering peanut butter and jelly kiss all over her face.

"You're so kind to share your sandwich with my face."

"You look funny mommy" he said, laughing himself silly.

Marlon learned early that if he made a mess, he should clean it up.

"Let me clean your face mom" he said licking Jolene's face all over laughing, and Jolene trying to escape the licking turning her head left and right.

"Just like dogs, see? you're clean."

"Are you going to spank me?" he asked with a sad serious face, believing his action deserved a spanking.

"No! I won't spank you."

"Cause I love you."

"Cause I love you, but that's not the way to clean people's face, only dogs do that.

"Why do they do that?"

"Because they don't have hands like we do."

"Oh yeah!" he agreed.

Turning to Joel, he made him an offer to share his sandwich. "Want to share my sandwich too daddy?

"No Marlon! Thank you. I don't want a licking too." Marlon laughed and laughed.

"And you know what Marlon?"

"What?" Marlon asked.

"God loves you too. He loves all of us."

"Do we love God mommy?

"Yes! we do, but we should love him more."

He sat silent on the floor with his train and plane, taking them apart, trying to see what makes them run and fly.

Suddenly he lifted his head and said quite soberly: "Mom you're beautiful and you're wonderful!"

Astonished at his words at three years old, Jolene realized how much impression she was making on him and vowed to preserve that image he perceives of her. To be careful with her words and deeds.

"Thank you, Marlon! I didn't know you think of me that way. You think I am beautiful and wonderful huh?

"Uh hu!"

Marlon was fast becoming more than daddy's buddy and mommy's big boy. He was raring to face the big world of mysteries and wonders.

CHAPTER

13

Joel's condition was gradually declining and started to take a toll on Jolene's mental and physical health. She was advised by her doctor to take some time away from the situation. Reluctantly, the decision was made for them to be separated just for a while.

Ruth, the younger of Jolene's two sisters had migrated to California in the United States. She wrote Jolene a most inviting letter in a sort of poetic form.

"Know what you need Big Sis?" it read. "You need a change of scenery and life-style.

To be where the lights are brighter, and the traffic moves faster. Where flowers of various kinds bloom in the spring, and the hills are so inviting, you think you can hear them sing.

We can go to San Francisco where little cable cars climb high, almost to the stars.

There is so much to see and do. Please come and bring Marlon too. I need to get acquainted with my nephew, since I missed the pleasure of watching my niece Marisa grow up."

How could she refuse such an invitation? How could she deny her sister the privilege of getting acquainted with her newest nephew?

Jolene accepted Ruth's invitation and within a month returned to the States with Marlon; this time to California leaving Joel in Aunt Agata's care.

Ruth escorted them around to get a quick glance and enjoy somethings of California. Travelling the scenic highways, they were amazed at the beautiful sceneries the hills displayed. In the cities, the prestigious high-rise buildings, hotels, hospitals, offices; the diversity of foods in the most welcoming restaurants; beautiful flower gardens everywhere; things they only heard about. Jolene and Marlon discovered that the lifestyle in California was completely different from Bluehole Cove island, and required adjustments that Jolene believed would not be a problem for them if they were to live there.

"Living in a country of opportunities and beauty, one could easily forget his problems at least for a while," she told Ruth.

"You can find opportunities that would encourage you and Marlon to stay and be a part of it all" Ruth assured her.

However, changing lifestyle was not easy for Marlon, he missed his father Joel, his Grandma Armenia, his friends, and especially his cousin Ralphie who he idolized. Ralphie took him places and did fun things that Joel was unable to do.

Accompanied by a family friend, Marlon returned home to Grandma Mini, his short for Armenia, since Joel was being taken care of by Aunt Agata and unable to take care of him, until he was ready to return to California to his mother. By then Jolene had fitted into the new life and had decided to make it her home.

Back home Grandma Mini carried him around to places she went, including the church a few blocks from the house.

Being a member of the choir, she would go to practice one night during the week and take Marlon with her. Not an interesting place for a then six-year-old, so, to pass the time there, he would equip himself with paper and pencil to draw for the ladies who seemed to like his artwork. To them he was a budding artist.

Failing that, he would go outside for different interests and new adventures. Next to airplanes, nature was always one of the many wonders to him, and at night, the stars were the most wonderful.

One practice night, bored and tired of drawing, he took off on one of his adventures, and for a breath of fresh air outside the church building. Down the steps and approaching the church yard, he stood focusing his attention on the stars and anything that caught his eyes. It was a quiet time of night when there wasn't much happening. People passing by occasionally, or a car now and then would make its way down the narrow street. Still admiring the stars, Marlon suddenly became overwhelmed with the feeling that he was being watched by someone, somewhere. Curiously, he turned and looked towards the church to see if anyone was around. No one was there, but from the corner of his eye he saw a figure that looked like an angel and turned his head to see what it was.

What he saw was a figure suspended aloft the church steeple; an illuminated form of an angel dressed in a conventional long white robe with long flowing wings protruding from its sides.

The entity had no visible end. Its robe seemed endless. The hue of the vision was a light-gold, almost white. It was obvious to him that the angel was of the feminine gender because to his knowledge an angel is a lady. Before he could get a good look at it, it was gone. She disappeared into the heavens within the twinkling of his eye, as if it were not intended for his eyes to witness her presence, and she had gotten caught. The entire experience lasted no longer than two second, but he would never forget it. He tried to describe all the events that led to his sighting to Grandma Mini.

Marlon always believed that he got a mere glimpse of his own, personal 'Guardian Angel.'

At birth he appeared to be healthy and strong, but before his sighting of the angelic form, he was afflicted with severe headaches. Greta, Jolene's older sister, took him to Doctor Moses Aguilara Pediatrician and explained his problem. He gave Marlon a thorough examination

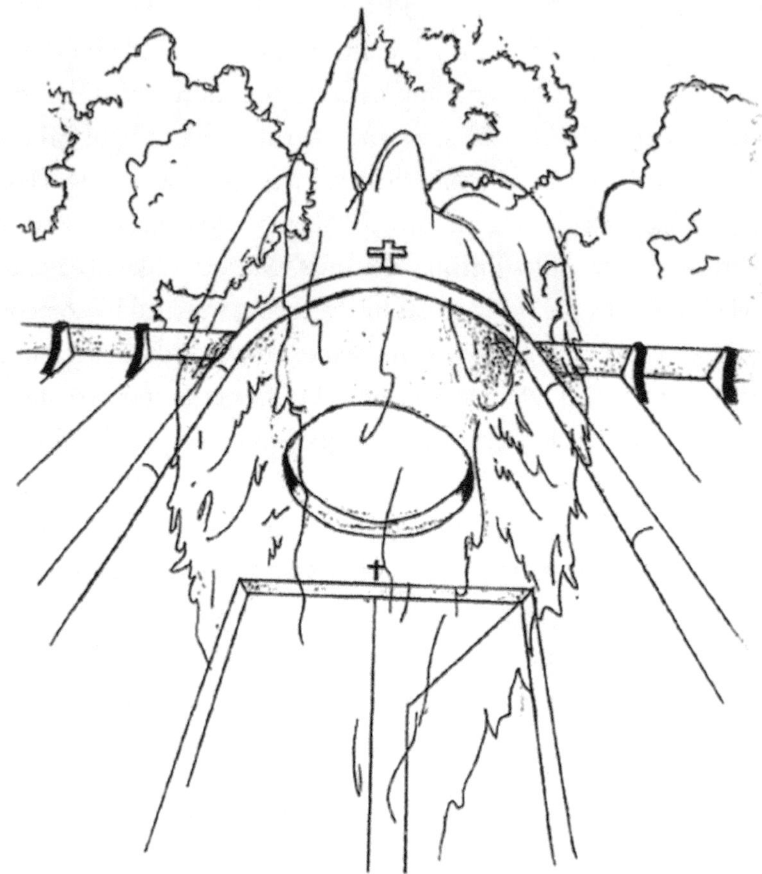

and concluded that it could be migraine headaches, but he was not convinced. A more extensive examination was necessary. He told Greta about the new medical inventions in the United States that could give

Marlon a more accurate examination and diagnosis. He advised Greta to informed Jolene of his condition and suggested that she make the necessary arrangements immediately to take him back to the States, where he could receive adequate medical attention and treatment.

Greta relayed the message to Jolene, and she was back on Bluehole Cove island in a hurry.

Marlon was all excited and ready to return with his mother, with the promise of seeing his father, his Grandma Mini and cousin Ralphie sometime soon.

From the minute he was reunited with his mother, Marlon did not stop telling her about the angel he had seen over the church. In Jolene's world, that was only fantasy in story books. She was not a believer of such things.

Marlon's headaches got worse, and Jolene took him to see several doctors; one told her the headaches will go away with time; another said some people get headaches after a plane flight.

Unfortunately, like Marisa's condition, the headaches came more frequently and more severe, he could not sit still, or lie down. All he could do was pace the floor screaming and holding his head.

The pain of watching another child agonize was back. In desperation Jolene quickly found the telephone book, a good source of information she thought. Going through the many pages of names of medical doctors and pediatricians she came across a name which was the same as his, only it was the doctor's surname and she thought he must be the one to help her child, so she made an appointment to see him.

Dr. Francis Marlon the pediatrician examined him and ordered tests and x-rays. With the advent of high-tech medical equipment's, it was much easier for problems to be detected. An arterial malformation of the brain was found to be the cause of Marlon's headaches. Surgery was the only answer, with the possibility of him becoming a vegetable with a slip of the doctor's hand. Fear once again struck Jolene.

"Was she about to lose this child also?"

CHAPTER
14

The date of the surgery was set to allow time for Joel to prepare to travel since he had become much better physically. It had been many years since Joel travelled anywhere, so he needed to make extensive preparations for his trip. He had to have a current passport and that takes at least a month to obtain; gathering all pertinent information to create the necessary documents for a passport. His medical condition had reduced him to a healthy medium size; therefore, a shopping expedition was necessary. To be away for any length of time, he had to be sure his medication was in order and sufficient to last until he was able to see a doctor.

All the preparations complete Joel said goodbye to Aunt Agata and boarded the local Cessna airplane leaving Bluehole Cove to make connection with one of the large international airlines flying to the United States. He left in high spirits anticipating the reunion with Jolene and Marlon.

Joel arrived in California in the height of the Christmas season, and fell right in line with the family rush to make it a grand Christmas. On Bluehole Cove island Christmas was celebrated in a unique way. For many people not having the finance to make early preparations, Christmas Eve was their busiest day. Some of the working ones were resigned to waiting until a day or two before Christmas for their boss to give them a Christmas bonus, then their shopping rush get underway.

Preparation would include painting the living room if it was needed; wash and paint or stain the wood floor and replace the covering whether it was carpet or linoleum, if it was worn out; the furniture were washed or scrubbed with sand paper to make them smooth and then varnished; window curtains were made and rush to hang as they came hot off the sewing machine; the children would have a good time washing pint bottles and getting each other all wet with balloon water bombs, the one thing that could be done early for the late preparers. The bottles were taken to the bottling factory to buy assorted fruit-flavor aerated drinks they call lemonade. Yes, they had to provide the pint bottles like a trade; they supplied the empty bottles, and the factory supplied the already bottled drinks. The menu was pretty much like Thanksgiving which included fresh turkey from the farm or in their yard for those who raised them, cured ham, rice-and-beans, potato salad, fried plantains, white pound cakes and black pound cakes made with burnt brown sugar, rum, or brandy, with or without cake fruits, assorted alcoholic beverages, and Rum Bumper.

Christmas would not be much good without a tree therefore, receiving the late bonus at the last minute, a tree, if they could find a good looking one, was bought and decorated with manufactured ornaments, as well as ornaments made by hand from shells and other things found on the island.

Church services were held on Christmas Eve celebrating the real meaning of Christmas, the birth of Jesus Christ. Hymns and carols rang out from the depths of their hearts and lungs. At the end of the service Christmas greetings and wishes are exchanged.

Some homes would have get-together with friends to drink 'den deh bram wid broom stick beat pan di flo ah wah mout ahgan. Then they dance to a beat on the floor made with a broom handle and a harmonica. Uninvited guests find their way into the celebration drinking and getting drunk. On Christmas day, small groups of African descendants travel from the southern parts of the island to the main city, to show some expression of their custom, dressed in African costumes or regalia.

The women wear a colorful and comfortably fitting blouse with streamers and strings of beads around their neck and arms, a head turban, a skirt fitting half-way to her ankles and bare feet. The men wear a colorful loosely fitting shirt with two long black sashes crossed on the chest, and loosely fitting pants, head dress with feathers, shells and some streamers, a mask covers the face, shells jangle around the arms and ankles, and bare feet. They dress and dance like Jankunu around the city, going from yard to yard, singing, or chanting with tum-tum drums beating an African beat, and patrons or on-lookers would throw money on the ground for them. They also danced on New Year's Day. With the celebrating over the matter of Marlon's surgery was discussed, being foremost in mind to be ready for that day.

Marlon was admitted in Christian Children's Hospital, in the children's ward at eight o'clock in the morning, prepared, and laid waiting to be taken to the operating room. Joel and Jolene were escorted to the waiting room to wait until the surgery was done.

Doctors Adam Clancy and Russell Roxbury introduced themselves and explained in layman's terms, the responsibilities and procedures of the surgery. They offered Joel and Jolene the opportunity to ask questions before Marlon was wheeled into the operating room.

"Periodically, a doctor will come to deliver a progress report. We are committed to do our best for Marlon" Doctor Clancy told them, hoping to increase their faith and ease their pain and anxiety.

Hour after hour they waited to hear from the doctors. To them it seemed like time stood still and the surgery was taking forever, not knowing how meticulous they had to be doing such a delicate job. A slip of the hand and he could become a vegetable the doctor had told them. Waiting was unbearable, but they prayed fervently for a successful surgery. Four o'clock in the evening before Dr. Clancy the operating surgeon, finally emerged from the operating room.

"Everything is fine! It went well!" he said. "We did as best we could under the circumstance. Had he been left any longer, it could have been fatal. Unfortunately, he will always have minor to moderate headaches from time to time, for the rest of his life."

He gave them a brief outline of the operation, but they did not fully understand, not having much knowledge of medical terms. They breathed a sigh of relief and thanked him and Doctor Roxbury for saving Marlon's life. Joel and Jolene thanked God for giving the doctors, nurses, and everyone that was involved, the wisdom, knowledge, strength, and courage to perform such an operation successfully to save Marlon's life. After all they only had one of him Joel would say. Their child was alive and well; he had endured eight hours of surgery; the doctors had done a fine job. Marlon was as normal as he was before, except for a ticking in his head which Doctor Clancy jokingly attributed to his watch left there during surgery. Occasionally, he would still experience less severe headaches.

The doctors and nurses who attended him were so good to him; they made his stay a pleasant one.

Teachers and children at Saint Augustine the school he attended, were also contributing factors to a pleasant stay in the hospital and his speedy recovery, by showering him with get-well cards they made at school, books, flowers, and stuffed animal presents.

Not having had experience with such a medical condition in any of the children before, Sister Margaret Michael, the principal of the school, thought it would be good for the students and teachers to do some studies on the brain. She invited Dr. Clancy the operating surgeon, to explain the wonders of the brain to the students and teachers of the three uppers classes as soon as Marlon was back in school. Well, that was not long. In two weeks, Marlon was ready to go back to school, although he was compelled to wear a cap to cover his clean-shaven head and scar from the surgery.

Dr. Clancy always took time from his busy schedule to work with students of all ages, especially those aspiring to pursue a profession in the medical field, therefore he graciously accepted Sister Michael's invitation and a date and time was set for his visit to the school. He arrived at Saint Augustine well equipped with visual aids and presented the 'whys and wherefores' of the activities of the brain to a captive audience of students and teachers. Dr. Clancy was very encouraged; he invited himself back for a follow-up session. Sister Michael too, was captivated with his talk and demonstrations, and assured him of his welcome to the school any time.

When it was all over, Jolene shuddered to think that she could have lost another child, had she not received Dr. Clancy's message from Greta to get him to the States and seek medical attention in time, but she also could not help thinking about his sighting of what he thought was his personal 'Guardian Angel', or maybe his Grandma Muriel Jennings who to him was his 'Guardian Angel' also, up in heaven like his sister Marisa.

The years passed and thoughts of the loss of Marisa waned. The consensus being that she died and was buried. Gone, but by no means forgotten, yet not to be dwelt on. That chapter of Jolene's life was still with unanswered questions.

CHAPTER

15

ne night Jolene had a dream, a beautiful dream. She dreamt her little baby girl had grown up. She had been raised by a family who lived in a large, lavishly decorated white house on Abyss Caye where she supposedly died. She looked about the age of seventeen years old. At the house where she was raised, the family was having a cocktail party, everyone with a drink in his and her hand, some sort of celebration. The guests were strange people, strange to Jolene and her son Marlon whom she did not remember being invited. They did not have a drink in their hand like the invited guests, which indicated that, 'where dogs are not invited, bones are not provided' nor drinks for that matter, but they were there all the same, and Marisa was happy with them being there as if she knew them, talking and laughing with Marlon. Among the seemingly well-to-do people, Jolene and Marlon looked very much like peasants dressed in ordinary unsophisticated clothes shoes and accessories.

From all observations, the party was in her, Marisa's honor. She looked so real, so pretty. She had a slim body about five feet tall, fair skin, black curly shoulder-length hair. She was wearing a blue background with white medium-size flowers dress. Her face was visible from the side only. Jolene's motherly instincts told her it was her daughter all right.

Jolene excused herself from their company and stood aside watching them having a good time as if they knew they were related to each other. She wished she knew what made them so happy, that made her happy too.

The dream was so real, when she woke up, she expected to see them both but there was only Marlon.

Jolene had never dreamt of Marisa before, so there had to be a meaning to her dream, and she was about to find out what it was.

Waking up to reality, Jolene was disappointed, but non-the-less happy to have had what she thought was an idea of what her daughter would have looked like.

A short while after such an awakening, she encountered sightings of a strange phenomenon.

Six o'clock in the morning was the regular time that Jolene would dress for work. One cool November morning was no different, except for what she discovered after showering. Never in her life was she so moved. The bathroom in their apartment was not fancy, nor could it accommodate a bathtub and shower. Everything was close at hand, and a full-length mirror which hung on the inside of the door, was one of them. Every time she turned around; she was face to face with herself. That morning, as she stepped out of the shower, she was not face to face with herself only, but on the mirror steamed from the heat of the shower was what looked like two-or-three-months old baby's footprints, almost from the top to the bottom. She showed them to Joel, and they were intrigued and curious, which later turned into concern. Her mind went wild trying to figure out how they got there.

Suddenly dreaming about Marisa; baby footprints appearing on the mirror; there had to be a meaning of some sort. She thought maybe somebody's baby was sick, or had died, so she called everyone she knew that had a baby; they were all doing well.

She invited the neighbors in the adjoining apartment to show them the strange prints on her mirror. She also invited a few family members to witness the unusual prints, and a friend whom she believed could interpret aberrations.

Coming up empty, her mind then went back to her baby, back to the days of her illness and death. She had to remind herself that the consensus was that Marisa had died, but even knowing how sick she was, curious and perhaps ridiculous questions popped into her head. "What if it were possible that she had survived that night; was treated and being released in somebody's care, but who? What then? I was only told that she died and was buried" she reminded herself. I did not see her in the coffin that was placed in the ground.

All the events of those four days spent on Abyss Caye started to flood her mind again, and for the first time since then, she took time to really review the whole series of events. She thought if she had to go to court for that matter, she could not swear that Marisa died, because she did not see her in the coffin that was buried, and she allowed guilt to step in blaming herself for not being more aware of the procedures of a funeral. However, it could have been different in that country.

She decided to reveal the events of the four days away to her family and a few friends. They thought she was dwelling too much on the past and should try to get on with her life. She did not tell anyone of the events of the death before, therefore no one knew what effect it had on her. For a long time, that was not foremost in her mind, hence the concern of the dream and the footprints. Jolene allowed the footprints to stay on the mirror for at least two weeks before cleaning them off.

A few days after the cleaning another set appeared in different formation. Those she let stay for some time and called up family and friends again, to let them know she was revisited by the strange --whatever. This time she became fascinated with the idea that maybe -just maybe it was her baby trying to communicate with her after all the time passed.

Remember, she was an unbeliever of such things, but it made her more comfortable believing that scenario.

One afternoon she cleaned the footprints off the mirror again and went to the kitchen to have lunch. She left the kitchen to wash up in the bathroom. When she returned the footprints were there again, even on one of the lockers and on the counter. Each time they appeared in different formation. Now she was a little bit scared. She was the only person in the apartment; it was getting too much; she was not comfortable anymore. She didn't know what to make of it. She took pictures and showed them to Pastor Jacob Mullins the Senior Pastor at the church they attended.

"Strange, isn't it? Do you think it has a meaning?" she asked.

"I've never seen anything like it before," he told her with a bewildered look.

"My poor baby's spirit must be wondering and has caught up with me" she lamented.

"You said you don't know for sure that she died; you didn't see her in the tiny coffin that was buried?

"Yes Sir! That is correct!"

"This is strange! Wish I knew what it means!"

Jolene's determination to find an answer was persuaded to seek help from a Parapsychologist. This was absolutely against her religion and her better judgment, but determination outweighed religion and better judgment, for this would weigh on her mind forever.

She spoke to one Parapsychologist who assured her that it was only juvenile energy being manifested. To her that meant that it had something to do with Marlon, the only juvenile in the apartment, but if so, what about the times when he wasn't around? That did not tell her much, so against her belief she decided to make an appointment to see a woman psychic, with whom her friend Karena was familiar.

Jolene and Joel met with the woman and with only the first two or three sentences of the story, and without the knowledge of the crux of the case, the woman went to work; her eyes shut tight; her hands clenched in a fist; her body motionless as if in a trance. Not a word spoken. This went on for at least ten or fifteen minutes, then rejoining her company, she opened her eyes, looked at Jolene and said:

"She is sick! and wherever she is, she needs you. You will have to try to find her. You will have another dream about her, when you do, come back to see me".

This was puzzling. Was she saying that Marisa was alive and was sick and needed her help?

Jolene left the woman's house, unsure if she should believe her or not. The idea of trying to find her baby was surely a good one, but not financially possible, therefore she had to find another way to get answers.

CHAPTER

16

The initiated correspondence through which she sought information. Letters concerning Marisa's death and burial went back and forth, trying to obtain information from the Abyss Caye Hospital and other areas, comparing notes of the actual times and manner of events, she was more baffled by the information she received.

For instance, she requested the medical records from the hospital and was told that it was not the policy of the hospital to release patient's medical records, not even to the parents of children.

Very odd she thought, and wrote another letter giving all the reasons why she needed them, but she tried in vain. All she was given was a letter that gave her a brief outline of Marisa's medical problems, as being fibrocystic disease of the pancreas, and information of findings in an autopsy that she did not request and was not told it was done. Not knowing the procedures of death and burial, none of it was enough to put Jolene's mind at ease. She had a need to know, and therefore decided to ask questions concerning the procedure of death announcements, autopsy, burial, death certificates and anything that is done in that event in that country.

Interestingly, all the answers received were not in accordance with the actual events as Jolene remembered them. Everything was done differently in that case, and what's more, she had to appeal to the government authorities for information, and to issue a death certificate. She later received a couple copies of the death certificate which stated a different time and date of death from the one issued by the hospital. This made her still more curious. What really happened? Was there a mistake made? or was it a case of 'the left hand not knowing what the right hand was doing'. Was she alive between those dates? If so, where was she all that time? Jolene wondered what she could do to get to the truth.

Returning to the scene now looked possible by compulsory, therefore arrangements were made, and a short flight landed Jolene back on Abyss Caye.

Arriving at the airport, and having retrieved her luggage, she was overjoyed when she turned around and found herself in the presence of Roger, a long-time friend who was equally happy to see her, and who, incidentally, was there on business of his own.

The greetings ended with the curious question of her presence there on Abyss Caye, which she explained briefly. Roger then offered to accompany her to the hospital and to assist in any way possible, having had some experience in research.

"With so many years behind this event, it probably will be difficult to find the people that were involved," she admitted to Roger, but she would not be deterred.

"Some people think that I should 'let sleeping dogs lie'; to forget it" but this dog does not need to lie, and my conscience will not allow that. I have a need to know" she told Roger. "I need to at least try to find answers."

After a brief introduction of herself and Roger to Miss Amy Allida the Hospital Administrator, Jolene, stumbling nervously over her words, tried to explain her mission.

"This might sound crazy" she said, "but, twenty-two years ago, I - my daughter was ill. She was sent from Bluehole Cove to this University Hospital for treatment. I do not know exactly what happened to her. I can't understand - I can't - I'm sorry" she concluded, tears rolling down her cheeks; her lips quivering as the memories crowded her head. Roger, trying to console her, took her in his arms and carried on the conversation, doing the best he could with what little Jolene had just told him. He explained that Marisa was there for treatment for cystic fibrosis, but that her stay was apparently short-lived since she was pronounced dead hours after arrival.

Jolene somewhat composed, went into the details. I was informed by Mrs. Harvey my hostess, who was informed by a police officer that she died. I was not asked to identify the baby's body for burial, nor was given an autopsy report then. I was not given a death certificate with a plot number. I can't even say with surety that she had died and was buried, because I didn't see her in the tiny coffin that was laid in the ground the following day, although I was there," she told them stifling a sob.

"I was not here at that time" Miss Amy Allida the hospital Administrator told them. She sympathized and promised to do a thorough investigation. Jolene was right about finding the same people in place.

Roger then suggested that they look for a burial plot while they waited for the Administrator's investigative report, but where would that be? Where would they look? Jolene had no idea of where the burial was. With so many natural disasters passing through the country over the years, looking for a burial plot with any remains, let alone specific remains was like looking for a needle in a haystack, but Jolene was determined to leave Abyss Caye with some sort of evidence, so they paid a visit to the City Council office.

"How may I help you?" A brusque voice from a fairly, large man with bulging eyes behind a rather large desk, inquired of Roger and Jolene. Their mission was presented, and another wait began.

Rummaging through some musty looking files, for fifteen or twenty minutes or so, the fairly, large man, chief clerk of the City Council office, perspiring profusely in the mid-summer heat, was becoming very disenchanted with the task set before him, since the search seemed fruitless.

"This is so ridiculous!" he grumbled under his breath. Jolene and Roger did not know what he meant; whether it was the idea of trying to find information from records of yesteryear, stored in such a haphazard manner, or the mid-summer heat, but with patience they waited, while the clerk became more and more aggravated.

"This will take some time to sort through!" he told them impolitely.

"You will have to come back in a week or so!"

"We don't have that kind of time" they protested.

"I'm afraid that's the best I can do just now." Jolene's frustration began to mount, but she kept on trying. Her next stop was Mrs. Harvey, her hostess for those four days twenty-two years ago. She did not have an address, or a phone number to call anyone. She didn't have any means of communicating with Mrs. Harvey and realized that she would have to seek diligently for her.

Jolene did search diligently, and her search revealed that Mrs. Harvey had retired from her job and sold her home to move into the GOD'S MERCY retirement home.

Twenty-two years had aged her immensely. Her hair was gray; her back humped over like she had the world sitting on her shoulders; her steps were slow, and her memory had faded as fast as her sight and hearing. There was no way of getting any information from her, and there was no one else Jolene knew that she could think of to contact, not even the friend that Mrs. Harvey claimed was expecting a baby and had asked for Marisa's clothes. She did not know who that friend was. Hope was not alive for that expedition.

One more disappointment, one more set-back. A Plan 'B' would have to be set in motion - 'Forensic Medicine.' After all the consensus, was that Marisa had died and was buried. Question was, where would they start and how would Jolene afford it? Would that government be willing and able to lend support to such an investigation?

A request was presented to the government to initiate a search for the remains, assuming there were remains, and DNA testing to be done at the University's Laboratory if found. That was a very unusual and difficult request, since Jolene was not asked to identify the body of her baby, and there was the question of whether she did die and was buried, and if so, where? After careful consideration, the government granted the request, and a search began.

With a ray of sunshine and a little hope in her heart Jolene thanked Roger again, and everyone that was involved. She returned home as empty as she did twenty-two years ago to wait for the results, and she did wait.

CHAPTER

17

Summer turned into fall and fall into winter which seemed like a never-ending season.

Then spring arrived and with it the long-awaited report of her findings. It read:

"We regret the long delay in reporting our findings to you. We did as extensive a search as was feasible, but because of the many natural disasters the country has experienced over the years, we were unable to locate documents or the exact burial site for your baby. Therefore, no remains were found. Our sincere regret and apology."

"It was worth a try" she consoled herself, and hurried a copy to Roger, still on assignment on Abyss Caye.

Considering her maternal instinct never revealed a loss to her, and the strange chain of events that followed her arrival in that country with her baby, she was unconvinced that an effort was made to search and entertained the thought that no site or remains were found, probably because nobody was buried.

"Faith has been unkind to me," she wrote to Roger, "but I'm exercising patience; that's on my side."

"The Administrator's promise to investigate must have fallen by the wayside. There hasn't been one word from her."

Within a month Roger replied to Jolene's letter to inform her of his research result.

"It will interest you greatly to know that in conversation with Miss Allida the Administrator, I learned that she is first cousin to Mr. Gambles the previous Administrator, who was present when you took the baby in; his sister Lillian is married to Mr. Uhuru the 'Loa Spirits' Guru that you visited up in the hills. He is a close friend of Mrs. Harvey. Small world that it is everybody is related to each other one way or another."

This information seemed to strike a nerve. Now suspicion tore at her heart, as she tried to put all the pieces of the puzzle together.

"Could it be that the Loa Spirits King's wife Lillian, was Mrs. Harvey's supposedly pregnant friend to whom all Marisa's clothes were given?" Probably not, they are well-to-do people and wouldn't need the clothes. After all the clothes were not receiving clothes, but bigger for a much bigger baby. She didn't think so but couldn't be sure. Her thoughts turned to the question of the big white house. Could it be that the Uhuru's big white house they visited was the one in Jolene's dream where Marisa lived? Somewhere in a remote area of her brain, Jolene had also harbored another thought that her baby might have been miraculously saved, removed from the hospital, and was alive somewhere. How and why that might have happened she hadn't a clue. The close family friend was a perfect setting for such transactions. Did something-of-that-sort of scenario happen? Could that be the reason she never heard from the Administrator? She was pondering all kinds of scenarios.

CHAPTER

18

For Jolene, a new project might be a good antidote for yet another failed attempt at finding answers, and the task of moving from the apartment to a house a few miles away in another city, though rough that might be, seemed like just the thing to do.

There was ample space in the house to accommodate additional bodies, and Jolene felt she was physically and mentally ready for a reunion with her mother Armenia Tradis also, who was aging and needed care. She therefore migrated to the United States to be with Jolene and her family.

There was much to be done in the house, unpacking and decorating, but now she had more help. Marlon was much older, bigger, and stronger, and Joel was still able to hang pictures and the famous mirror. They kept it as a memorial of Marisa's life, placed on the inside of the bathroom door just like it was at the apartment. Incidentally, the bathrooms in the house were not much more than the one in the apartment, so they were still face to face with themselves to every turn, making Jolene's self-inflicted, self-image being plump, lash out at her, begging to be reprieved.

Whatever it was lurching in the apartment, was not about to be left behind.

After being in the house a month or so, tiny footprints appeared again on the mirror.

Somehow Jolene was always the first to discover them, probably the reason for her to believe it had something to do with her baby. They were all puzzled by the persistence of the strange phenomenon.

Not being able to watch his mother struggle with the wonderment of this phenomenon, Marlon thought it might help if he could convince her that it is possible to make the prints by hand and proceeded to explain and show how one of the children at school, back in his sixth-grade class told him how to make footprints on a mirror.

"Make a fist!" he said "press the bottom side on to the mirror and use your fingers to make little toes. The mirror must be steamed up for the prints to show. One day I made them just to try it," he said with the utmost sincerity, "but now they keep coming back. I did not make anymore, and do not know how or why they keep coming back, even after you clean them off. I know it wasn't me making them mom" he confessed to his mother.

"They came back even when you were not at home, so it couldn't be you then" Jolene assured him.

"Knowing you were contented with the idea that it probably was my sister Marisa trying to communicate with you, I thought there was no need to discourage you."

He was so thoughtful. Sure, she was comfortable with them; curious but comfortable. We were all comfortable after a while.

"Whatever it was that moved with us, had a mind of its own" Joel told the family. Not only did little footprints appear in this house, but little handprints also appeared a couple times, after Marlon's clear explanation and confession. It was obvious that it couldn't be Marlon making them. After all he was much bigger, much older, and much more matured for such childish pranks. He was now into things like art, entering art contests winning blue ribbons and prizes.

After this discovery, Jolene found herself wishing there was a face to go along with those prints of hands and feet, but there wasn't one. She cleaned them off and they never returned. How and why, she had no idea. She wished she knew what it all meant.

The parapsychologist was right about one thing if nothing else. Even though she did not say when, Jolene did dream about Marisa again. This time she dreamt a taxi stopped at her gate and Marisa stepped out. It appeared she had just arrived from the airport or train station. Jolene did not recognize her at first site and therefore she did not rush to greet her. She was wearing the same blue and white dress, looking the same as she did in her first dream.

Marisa turned around to retrieve her luggage from the back seat of the taxi, instead of allowing the driver who was walking toward her side to assist her. Before she could take them out, Jolene again woke up to the harsh reality of it being just a dream.

The psychic woman had told Jolene to report any more dreams to her, but she vanished from the area, therefore Jolene was left to form her own interpretation of 'she is sick and needs you'.

CHAPTER

19

Word of the physical condition of Jolene's nine-year-old niece Angelica needing medical treatment that was not available on Bluehold Cove island, reached Jolene and Joel, and they were obliged to assist Angelica, to bring her to the Unites States for whatever treatment was necessary, not equating the situation to the psychic woman's vision of Marisa being sick and needed her.

Angelica arrived in the United States accompanied by her mother Elodia. They were so tired from the long flight clear across the world, and Angelica not being her best self, Joel drove them straight home to rest.

The following week Angelica was seen by a Specialist at the Christian Hospital, who ordered tests and x-rays for her. The results clearly showed the need for surgery. Three bones in her back were inclined to overlap, the reason she was in the early stage of scoliosis. She was admitted in the hospital and surgery was scheduled for the week ahead.

Being shy and away from home in a strange place with strange people, it was difficult for Angelica to adjust, but the staff and children in the hospital were kind and friendly; they helped her to adjust, and it did not take long for her to fall in place with the other children. More tests and x-rays were done before surgery was performed.

Elodia her mother, said a short prayer for a safe and successful surgery while she, Joel and Jolene waited patiently for it to be over. Like Marlon's surgery one of the doctors came out intermittently to give a progress report and assure them that all was going well.

Recuperation was the next phase of her treatment, starting with therapy, and learning to maneuver herself in a wheelchair to stay mobile. To her that was fun wheeling around with the other wheel-chair-bound children. She was well adjusted. Joel, Jolene and Elodia, and sometimes Marlon visited her often to monitor her progress and assure her that they will always be there if she needed them.

To make her stay more pleasant, she received gifts from visiting local celebrities. She was happy. Her one complaint was that the nurses woke her up 'too much to give her medicine'. Once she pinched the nurse for waking her up.

Within three weeks Angelica recuperated enough to be released from the hospital. Preparing to take her home Elodia and Jolene packed her clothes, shoes, and pillows to make her comfortable for the long eighty-five miles ride home while Armenia, Jolene's mother, helped to pack the snacks and juices; orange juice, especially for Joel to keep his blood sugar in order. Marlon's contribution to her home coming was a 'WELCOME HOME' cartoon poster he made. They all did what they could to make her experience a good and memorable one, and it would be memorable indeed.

Joel was the only driver on that trip. On the way back from the hospital he decided to show Elodia and Angelica something of the city. He had been driving for a while showing and explaining things to them. His blood sugar went low, and his driving started to swerve on the streets. Jolene and Marlon recognized the signs of his blood sugar depleting, and he was about to go into diabetic shock. They quickly tried to force him to drink a glass of orange juice, which was never an easy task. They could not get him to drink, and he kept on driving at thirty-five miles. Jolene sitting next to him tried to take the steering wheel, while keeping an eye out for a Police Officer, but not even one was in sight. Jolene became so desperate, she thought to knock him out, but could not do it, so they kept going praying somebody would help them.

They had never had such an experience, and they were very afraid they would have an accident, like the premonition Elodia had in a dream she told Jolene about just minutes before. His swerving got worse; he was going all over into other lanes. Fortunately, living on that small island there never were much traffic on the streets; it was a quiet time except for Angelica crying and screaming in fear.

"I noh wah get hurt ah go back da hospital" - "I don't want to get hurt and have to go back to the hospital" she kept screaming. Armenia was in tears; her heart racing; her breathing heavy. Jolene was afraid she would have a heart attack again right then. Elodia panicking, prayed out loud to God for help.

Jolene prayed fervently in silence while Marlon took a turn trying to stop the car. God heard their prayers, and somehow, they were able to make Joel drink enough orange juice to stabilize his blood sugar. He regained composure and they arrived home safely. It was certainly a most frightening, unforgettable experience.

Within a month, Angelica was well enough for her mother to return home to the rest of her family, leaving her to remain on Bluehole Cove Caye with Jolene to receive further treatment. Although she was not considered a replacement for Marisa, the relationship between Jolene and Angelica became like mother and daughter. Incidentally, Angelica was born in the same month, four days after Marisa's birthday and there were, semblance of each other. Jolene imagined that Marisa probably would have done some things the way Angelica does; would have liked some things Angelica likes, especially parties; her mood-swings would have been much like Angelica's moods, so it was just like having Marisa. Her interpretation of her dreams and sightings was that of Angelica's presence in her home. Jolene enrolled Angelica in grade school, and she went on to graduate from High School.

She had grown into an enterprising young woman, ready to take on the world. Very clever in the kitchen creating all sorts of cakes and pastries. With much encouragement from friends and family to pursue a career in the art, she enrolled in a baking class in the day, and a business class at night. Graduated with an Associate degree, she was preparing herself for a challenge to compete in the business world. She recognized the importance of financial resources to meet that challenge and hired herself out, to work as an apprentice in a large baking establishment. She became very proficient to the point of upgrading to Head Baker in the space of three years. Quite an achievement at her young age. Her goal then, was to reach for the title "Owner", which she did, and named it DULCY'S DELIGHS. Her business prospered and became quite famous.

CHAPTER 20

Next to Christmas, Thanksgiving was Joel's favorite event. His birthday didn't mean much to him after fifty. He used to say birthdays after fifty are mere anniversaries.

Anyway, Thanksgiving was the upcoming event, and he volunteered to prepare the feast, good cook that he was. Family and friends had always enjoyed his cuisines. The menu was carefully planned. The shopping was done early in the week before. The turkey he seasoned and stored until the big day. Everything was set to go.

Early one morning as Jolene prepared for work, Joel still sleeping, started a telephone conversation with one of his cousins.

"Hello!" he said. Then a short silence, his eyes still closed. "This is Joel!"

Another short silence as if the person on the other end was answering and he was listening. He sat up still pretending to be listening.

"Oh, hi Dorothy! I'm not too well these days, but better than I was not long ago." Then there was another short silence.

"Here Jolene, talk to her!" he said sitting on the edge of the bed, this time with his eyes open, his arm stretched out to Jolene as if he was passing the telephone to her.

Jolene stretched out her arm also, pretending she was receiving it. "Hello!" she said, not knowing with whom she was talking invisibly.

"This is Jolene! How are you doing?" Then a short silence just the way Joel did.

"I'm fine but rushed getting ready to go to work. Sorry, I'll have to talk with you again some other time. Talk to Joel!"

"Here!" She pretended to pass the phone to Joel still sitting on the edge of the bed.

"I have to go now, Dorothy. Goodbye!" he said. "Goodbye. I have to go." He continued. "You can hang up!"

"I have to go!" he said a third time, as if the other person was unwilling to end the conversation.

"You can go now; I'll see you soon!" Jolene at this point intervened.

"He has to go now, Dorothy. Say goodbye!" she said and pretended to hang up.

Joel politely laid down, closed his eyes and in a minute, he was snoring.

During dinner, Jolene remembered the strange conversation she and Joel had before she left for work that morning.

"Who was that we talked to this morning while I was getting dressed to go to work?"

"What are you talking about?"

"This morning you and I talked to a person you called Dorothy." she told him.

"The only Dorothy I could think of is my cousin, but she's been dead for thirty-five years."

Jolene became uneasy. They were conversing with a deceased cousin. It was the belief that dead relatives visited their loved ones before they were taken away.

Two days before Thanksgiving Day, Dorothy must have returned because Joel passed away in the middle of preparing the turkey dressing. Thanksgiving Day came, and the family gathered as usual for dinner albeit in a noticeably somber mood. However, everyone tried to make conversation, even managed a laugh or two without feeling guilty eating turkey and cranberry with long faces.

With Thanksgiving behind them Jolene made all the preparations and arrangements for Joel's burial with the help of her family.

"When we met," Jolene said to a gathering of friends and family members who had come to share the last moments with them, "I prepared the Thanksgiving dinner which we quietly enjoyed. Now he was preparing Thanksgiving dinner that he will never finish and enjoy."

Joel was laid to rest at a Military cemetery.

Jolene was now a widow, left with Marlon and Angelica to carry on.

CHAPTER
21

Years later, Marlon all grown up, found himself in the marrying category for men, having found Paulene Saintly a beautiful, well rounded figure, quite mannerly and intelligent young lady, a native of Scotts Cove Caye, his 'soul mate' for life he thought. Their relationship flourished for two years, and they believed they were quite compatible, both accustomed to the same culture; the same kind of foods and entertainment, same values and beliefs, worshiped the same God, and enjoy the same kinds of weather and music. Marlon decided that their relationship was established enough for them to become engaged and get married. Paulene agreed readily, she didn't want to wait longer. She was afraid her biological clock was running out of time. Marlon ordered a ring for her with pearls setting from his home as a symbol of their engagement. The wedding was planned to be six months later. Simple but elegant, with solemn traditional vows it would be. With the help of their families, preparations got under way.

Invitations were sent out to family and a few friends it read:

Mr. and Mrs. Philip Saintly request
the pleasure of your company
to the marriage of their daughter
Pauline Saintly to Marlon Jennings

son of Mrs. Joel Jennings
on Saturday October 5, 1995
to be held at the Hill and Valley Hotel

Paulene's parents Mr. and Mrs. Phillip Saintly and her only brother Paul Saintly were flown in from the island a week before to spend some time making acquaintance with Marlon and his family.

Marlon and Pauline met them at the airport and with handshakes and hugs they greeted each other.

"We're happy to meet you. We've heard so much about you from Paulene, we feel like we've known you always; what a gentleman and how family oriented you are" Mrs. Saintly said to him.

"Thanks for that nice compliment Paulene, I do try. Sorry I don't have both parents for you to meet. My father Joel passed away a few years ago" Marlon apologized.

"We're sorry son, it would have been good to have him at your side at this time" Mr. Saintly told him.

"I'm sure he would have been proud, watching you launch out to face this crazy world with confidence and maturity" Mrs. Saintly added to the condolence.

"Thank you. It would have been good to have him with me.

"Who is standing with you then?" Mr. Saintly asked.

"Oh, my cousin Ralph who has been my big brother all my life has agreed to accompany me.

"I see!"

With the greetings over, Marlon decided it was time to move on to the house.

"We will go to our house to grab a bite and rest" he suggested. Jolene arrived just as they were about to leave the airport. More hugs and kisses and greetings were displayed, while Marlon loaded their luggage in the trunk of the car, then they all left for Jolene house.

Jolene had prepared a light lunch of turkey and cheese, ham and cheese sandwiches, green salad, and sweet potato pone dessert, with pineapple lemonade to wash it down. Marlon served Mr. Saintly an aperitif, a sip of Rum Bumper to wet or stimulate his appetite. Delightfully filled they moved on to conversations and organization of the wedding.

"Are you or Marlon having second thoughts or getting nervous yet Paulene?" Jolene asked.

"I'm not" Paulene told her.

"Not so far" was Marlon answer, then a brief silence.

"All goes well, next week this time I'll be your mother-in-law Paulene, and your parents will be Marlon's mother and father-in-law Jolene said, trying to keep the wedding mood intact.

"That's right!" Mrs. Saintly agreed.

"If you, parents, mom and dad and Jolene will be our in-laws, what will you be to each other?" was Paulene's curious question.

"I don't know who first decided that our parents will be our mother and father-in-law, but somebody did, but they didn't decide what our parents will be to each other. I think they would be kins-in-law, don't you?" Marlon asked Paulene.

"I never thought of that relationship before. I never knew how to regard their relationship to each other, but that makes sense to me."

Still following in his father's footsteps Marlon enlisted in the Air Force because of his love for airplanes. He was always fascinated with military uniforms and activities and found the perfect opportunity to wear one, and to participate in military activities serving his country. The wedding planner incorporated that in the wedding plans with a small twelve-men military arch formation, leading up the steps to the Hill and Valley Hotel ballroom, honoring his father, the late Air Force Colonel Joel Jennings.

A beautiful wedding was catered by a creative wedding planner: Flowers, candles, ribbons, bells, and ornaments all over the small, rented ballroom. Aroma of various kinds of island foods filled the room; quite inviting. An array of imported, exotic drinks was on the menu along with the famous national drink 'Rum Bumper.'

The preparations, the ceremony, everything went well without any glitches, except a minor error in the music arrangement which was to be a medley of island dance music and contemporary music for dining and dancing but was erroneously replaced with jazz. The planner quickly remedied the situation and dance lovers including the parents, took to the floor showing off their dance moves and having a good old time, but it seemed like weddings in that family were not to be without surprises, and this one was no different, it had a surprise that really gave credence to its meaning.

Being residents of the same small village in Jennah, Naida, Joel's friend, had become acquainted with Hannah, Joel's previous wife. She was also acquainted with the fact that Hannah had conceived and gave birth to a daughter she named Sarah, fathered by Joel, but deliberately canceled it from him, depriving him of the joy of fatherhood. Her reason being that she could no longer take care of Joel and would leave him, and she did. Still a young child Sarah was made aware of the facts and vowed to find her father as soon as she was old enough to do so.

In conversation with Naida once, Sarah had gathered enough information to initiate a search. Since Naida's contact with Joel was many years before, she would have to make persistence her guideline for her success, but at least she had an idea where to start. Obviously, she didn't know how, when or where her search would end.

CHAPTER

22

After many months of phone calls and letters to military and political figures, both at home and in the United States, Sarah was given an address in San Francisco in the United States to look for Mr. Claud Jex, the owner of the Hill and Valley Hotel who knew her father, Joel Jennings. She left her home in Jennah and travelled across the miles to find that address. Coincidentally, her search led her to the Hill and Valley hotel high on a hill with views looking down and around, she thought it to be one of the most beautiful scenery of nature God has made. A combination of orange hue and blue lined sky behind green hills, tall green trees of every kind, mingled with light fog hovering over a row of beautiful houses.

She alighted the taxi she hired for the search, climbed a few steps of the building, gingerly opened the door not knowing what to expect to find inside but she discovered soon enough.

Inside the hotel were elegant furnishings, soft Persian carpet floors everywhere, custom draperies, beautiful flowers and expensive ornaments to name a few obviously expensive articles, mouth-watering flavors filled the air; scrumptious living was indicated.

"Good evening, welcome to Hill and Valley, I'm Lacelle at your service," a most polite young bellhop with a very enchanting smile introduced himself.

"Thank you!" she told him and stepped up to the desk to check into the hotel.

"Welcome to Hill and Valley!" the clerk at the desk echoed welcoming her too. "May I help you?"

"A room with bed to rest my tired body would be just fine" she told him.

"It's already waiting for you."

The clerk gave the keys to the bellhop and instructed him to take Sarah to her allotted room.

After resting and refreshing herself, Sarah went back to the desk to enquire about the owner she was to contact who knew Joel well.

"Excuse me please, where would I find Mr. Claud Jex owner of this establishment" she asked the clerk.

"Go back towards the front door, turn left to the main entrance you will find Mr. Claud Jex in his office.

"Thank you, sir" she said and proceeded to find Mr. Jex.

Undecided on what she should say to Mr. Jex, Sarah stood outside his door for a few minutes, thinking. She decided to just tell him who she is and the reason for her call on him, so she picked up the courage and knocked on the door.

"Come in" a masculine voice answered. Sarah opened the door and was greeted with a smile and a handshake.

"I'm Sarah Jennings, Joel Jennings' daughter she said shyly. I was told to search for you because you know my father very well and you might have an idea where I can find him. I didn't have the pleasure of knowing him. I came here to San Francisco in hopes of finding him"

"Joel's daughter huh! Oh yes! We know each other well he told her not knowing of Joel's death. Had some great times in the Military partying, travelling, getting in all sorts of mischief, but never any trouble. He was wounded and was put on the disabled list to return home. Haven't seen him since."

"Did you know my mother too?"

"Oh yes, a fine lady but wasn't able to care for your father for too long." "There is much more I can tell you about him, but this is not the best time to do so. We will have to meet again for the rest of my knowledge of him. Good old 'Boots'.

"Boots? why boots?"

"His military name. Always wore shine boots.

"I'll have to remember that when I find him, Sarah said with a smile.

"Very well, I will look forward to that. Thank you very much Mr. Jex." With hope in her heart Sarah hurried to leave the building. Passing a small ballroom, she was surprised to find a celebration going on, but was too excited about her good fortune in finding the address and Joel's friend Mr. Jex, to find out what the occasion was. However, the beautiful wedding decorations indicated the event that became obvious to her one-track mind, and she just had to invite herself in to enjoy seeing the beautiful, elegantly dressed guests, and hear the sweet sound of island music. She so loved weddings and island music just like Ruth, Jolene's little sister.

As an uninvited guest and a stranger, she waited for an opportunity to explain her presence.

Recognizing a stranger in their midst, Marlon took time away from his bride to speak to her. Sarah apologized to him for the intrusion, and fearing a missed opportunity, explained to him that she was on a mission to find her father Joel Jennings, and that was the address she was given to find him. That of course was astonishing. The most unbelievable story if ever he heard one, not to mention how wrong her timing was.

That certainly was neither the time nor place for such a surprise, but curious now, he engaged in a rather delightful conversation, laughing at intervals.

Sarah's features were much like Joel's: black hair, grayish eyes, olive skin, slender, about five feet two inches tall. In a blue background floral dress almost like the one in Jolene's dream with matching shoes and bag, not exactly a formal wedding ensemble, but very becoming, she turned heads, including Jolene's from a distance.

The scene of Sarah and Marlon talking and laughing happily, was quite familiar to Jolene though she didn't know why. The woman looked familiar. She was sure she had seen her before.

After hearing Sarah's story, Marlon sought his mother and cousin to introduce Sarah with her amazing mission. Not being in the right place at the right time, they discussed the preface of the mission and Jolene invited Sarah to spend some time at her home so they can go into details. Mr. and Mrs. Marlon Jennings were also invited to dinner and join in the discussion.

It was late in the night; Sarah hired a taxi to return to the Hill and Valley Hotel to get her belongings and return to Jolene's home. When she reached the hotel, she quickly retrieved the keys from her purse in readiness to enter her room. She inserted the key in the door lock, turned it, the door opened, she entered in and was instantly confronted by a drunk man with a butcher's knife, wheeling round and round in the air, threatening her life and demanding all the cash she had. Fearing for her life she hurriedly gave him every penny she had, except for a dollar she had hidden in another pocket in her purse. Thankfully, he was satisfied and left the room leaving her trembling with fear.

As soon as she was calm, she reported it to the clerk who was unaware of the intruder and reported to the police. Obviously then, she was engaged in lengthy questioning and interviews. Not a nice experience for her first visit she thought. She told Jolene of her scare and Jolene offered her sanctuary for the duration of her time in the country, but Sarah declined convincing Jolene that she would be just fine.

The following day she returned to Jolene and helped her to prepare the dinner. Marlon and Paulene provided drinks and desserts. When dinner was over, they retreated to the family room where Jolene initiated the conversation with pictures of Joel, and with Marlon's help, gave Sarah the history of her father's life and death as they knew it.

With much regret for all the lost time, Sarah explained that her job as a dress designer and buyer kept her busy, and not being in one place long enough to concentrate on a search. They sympathized with her for not getting the chance to know the most gracious and loving father that she had.

Sarah was happy with the partial success of her mission and the discovery of her brother, but sadly disappointed in not finding her father alive. She kept her promise to see Mr. Jex for more information on her father and informed him of his death.

Marlon took Sarah to the cemetery to Joel's grave site before she returned home to Jennah. They promised to stay in touch so they can get to know each other, and for Paulene to know her new-found family including her sister-in-law, Sarah.

Mr. and Mrs. Marlon Jennings celebrated their first 'Paper' Anniversary, with a little bundle of joy on the way to carry on the next generation of Jennings.

Five years has flown by amazingly fast, now they are celebrating their 'Wood' anniversary.

"You are now seasoned married people and seasoned parents" Sarah wrote to them. "I shall have to return someday to make acquaintance with your offspring".

"Here's wishing you a Happy Anniversary." Sarah sent her anniversary congratulations to the happy couple with a song she made that says:

Happy anniversary to you
You kept your vows and promises true
Hope you'll be happy next year too
Happy anniversary to you

"Paulene can play it on her keyboard being the musician." The thought of their happiness made her lonely.

For many years Jolene could think of not much more than the scene of Marlon and Sarah in a happy conversation, wondering when, where and if indeed there was ever such a scene before. Then one day it became clear to her. She remembered.

"Of course!" she said to herself. "It was my dream long ago, of Marlon and Marisa happily engaged in conversation at a celebration at somebody's white house. "This is the real interpretation" she conceded. "After all Sarah is Marlon's half-sister."

At first, she thought that the dream and footprints on the mirror meant the presence of Angelica her niece, being like a daughter in her home, but now believes that they were merely to alert her of Angelica's need for help. She contented herself with those two reasons to put her mind more at ease from the loss of Marisa. However, there still has not been any concrete proof of Marisa being dead and buried, or that she was treated and miraculously survived and is alive somewhere, but Teddy her teddy bear friend was still around and was passed on to her cousin Emily to enjoy.

Have you ever had any of those experiences? If you have not, are you convinced that some do happen, maybe not in the exact way, for example, Jolene's 'dream' of Marlon and Marisa in conversation at the white house which actually turned out to be Marlon and Sarah, his half-sister. Then Marisa's homecoming which was, as the Psychic woman told Jolene her daughter was sick and needed help, that was actually Angelica going to the United States with her mother Elodia, who also had a 'dream' of them having an accident taking Angelica home from the hospital, and that almost happen.

Joel and Jolene's 'invisible conversation' with Joel's deceased cousin Dorothy, and Joel's passing soon after, the 'omen' that being visited by a deceased relative is a sign of imminent passing of someone in the family. Marlon's angel was quite possibly an 'illusion' but very real to him possibly saving him from a disastrous surgery.

There is also an 'old wives' tale' that says if a baby is born 'too pretty,' it would not live.

A 'superstition' that if two women being pregnant, which Jolene and her friend Maggie were, and one delivers her baby, the other should not go to see the baby because one of the babies would die. Well Maggie, Jolene's friend, delivered her baby and Jolene did visit her. Unfortunately, Marisa was presumed to have died but Jolene believed that was a mere coincident.

Not forgetting the 'phenomenon' of the 'Footprints on the Mirror' which was merely Marlon's curiosity to prove his friend's theory of making footprints on a mirror, that caused Jolene to truly realize the loss of Marisa.

Jumping through hoops seeking some answers, Jolene wondered if she would ever know what really happened to her baby girl and would eventually be at peace with herself.

THE END

9.951   48288CB00009B/3094   [217365352]